A BLUE WATER DEATH

James P. Maywar

iUniverse, Inc.
New York Lincoln Shanghai

A Blue Water Death

Copyright © 2006 by James Maywar

iUniverse books may be ordered through booksellers or by contacting:

iUniverse
2021 Pine Lake Road, Suite 100
Lincoln, NE 68512
www.iuniverse.com
1-800-Authors (1-800-288-4677)

ISBN-13: 978-0-595-37216-4 (pbk)
ISBN-13: 978-0-595-81614-9 (ebk)
ISBN-10: 0-595-37216-3 (pbk)
ISBN-10: 0-595-81614-2 (ebk)

Printed in the United States of America

For Nancy—thank you for your boundless love and support.

Acknowledgments

Most of the information about the United States in 1913 was found in the following sources: *The 1910's* by David Blanke, *Victorian America: 1876–1915* by Thomas J. Schlereth, *America's Women* by Gail Collins, *The Timetables of History* by Bernard Gunn, *Twentieth Century Fashions* by Valerie Mendes and Amy de la Haye, *Casebook of Forensic Detection* by Colin Evans, *History of the Michigan State Highway Department: 1905–1933* by Frank Rogers, and *When Eastern Michigan Rode the Rails: Book Two* by Jack Schramm and William Henning.

Most of the information about Port Huron in 1913 was found in the following sources: 1913 issues of the *Port Huron Times-Herald*, the Michigan Room of the St. Clair County Library, *A Story of Port Huron* by Helen Endlich, *Tunnel Tales* by Wanda Pratt, and *An Enduring Heritage* by Keith Yates.

The dedicated and courteous staff at iUniverse converted my story into a novel.

Todd Gustavson, Elwin Hartwig, Bob Irving, Dick Klaus, Wendy Krabach, Marcy Kuehn, Nancy Nyitray, Bill Pierce, Gordon Ruttan, Jim Warner, and reference librarians at the St. Clair County Library and the Michigan Law Library helped me with my research.

George and Sharon Marie Joachim, Donna Maywar, and Catherine and Ed Moore proved their friendship by reading an early draft and offering helpful suggestions.

My son Drew Nelson Maywar, lowered my blood pressure by solving the case of the missing file, and other puzzling computer mysteries.

My son Eric James Maywar, demonstrated his excellent skills by patiently editing several versions of the story, and providing invaluable advice.

My wife, Nancy, cheerfully read the material, and provided enthusiastic support.

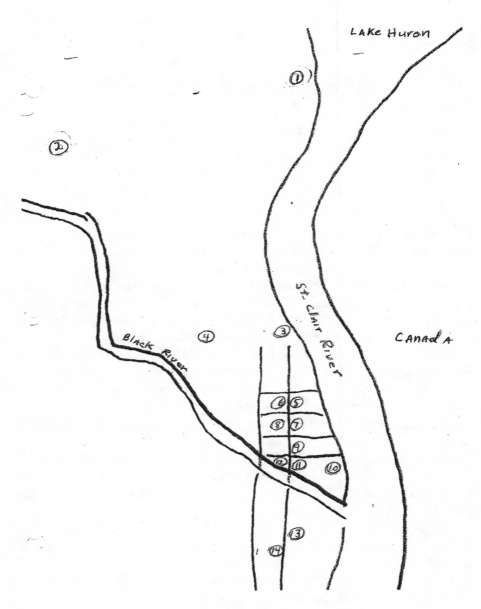

Map of Port Huron

Tobias Sharpe's Port Huron—1913

1. Fort Gratiot Lighthouse

2. Driving Park

3. Pine Grove Park

4. Mrs. Jenkins' boardinghouse

5. *Port Huron Star* newspaper office

6. Maccabees' building

7. Hotel Marion

8. Port Huron police department

9. Fisherman's Tavern

10. Velvet Cushion's house of pleasure

11. Sperry's department store

12. Majestic Theater

13. Harrington Hotel

14. Price Albert Hotel

PROLOGUE

─────────── ▼ ───────────

Patrolman Wilbur Greene's nerve-racking cackle permeated the police station main office. "You mean to tell me that professional football will become as popular as baseball?"

Patrolman Tobias "Toby" Sharpe cleared his throat. "I didn't say it would be. I said it might be. Football's popular in high schools and colleges. Maybe someday pro ball will become popular too."

Wilbur smirked. "Every time someone tries to organize a professional football team, it flops."

"The same thing happened in baseball fifty years ago."

"But how can someone make a living playing just ten or twelve games a year?"

Toby said, "Things change. Maybe someday businessmen will figure out how to make professional football work."

"Things change? Is that your flimsy explanation? Take my word for it—nothing's ever going to replace baseball, boxing, and horse racing as America's favorite sports."

Toby opened his mouth to respond but decided not to say anything. He stood up and put on his hat. "Looks like it's time to go home."

Wilbur asked, "You want to go to Fisherman's Tavern for a couple of drinks? You could tell me more stories about social change."

"No thanks. I want to go home to my family."

Wilbur cackled again. "You sure got stuck with a heavy ball and chain. I guess that's one thing about marriage that's never going to change."

Toby's face flushed. "You know Greene, if that's what you think marriage is like, it's a good thing you're single."

Toby hurried to the trolley stop. Once on the trolley, Toby replayed the conversation with Wilbur Greene. At twenty-five, he was only one year younger than Wilbur, but Toby always thought Greene treated him as a kid. Toby understood that part of the problem was his reluctance to argue.

He knew that changes in science, transportation, entertainment, and the role of women made the United States a much different place in 1913 than twenty-five years ago. But if he tried to talk about any of this to Wilbur, it would just be made into a joke.

Toby was not interested in all types of change. He smiled as he remembered when a high school teacher tried to explain Einstein's theory of relativity, and Toby's eyes just glazed over. The only thing he remembered about the lecture was what happened when the teacher circulated a photograph of Einstein. One girl said he was cute, and his best friend, Bill Boyd, made the class laugh for saying he thought it was Dr. Frankenstein.

What really interested him were the recent changes in land transportation. The first bicycle was manufactured in the United States in 1878. Within a few years, bicycling became very popular. By 1900 many people, including Toby, had bicycles. He caused his mother considerable grief that year when he, Bill Boyd, and several friends rode their bicycles to the village of Marysville without getting permission.

Also by 1900, electric trolleys, called interurbans, connected many cities. When baseball owners established the American League in 1901, Toby and his dad would take the interurban from Port Huron to Detroit to see the Tigers play at Bennett Park. The park was named after Charley Bennett, a major league catcher who lost both of his legs in a train accident in 1894. Bennett played for the Detroit Wolverines, a National League franchise in the 1880s. Bill Boyd did some calculations and concluded that Toby must have been conceived on the day the Wolverines won the National League pennant in 1887.

Like many Americans, Toby was amazed when the Wright brothers flew the first airplane. He wondered how it managed to stay in the air and occasionally thought that maybe he should have paid more attention in science class.

It was the development of the automobile, however, that currently captured Toby's attention. Until recently, he could only dream about owning a motor car. But when Henry Ford's assembly line techniques dramatically lowered prices, automobiles became more accessible. Toby hoped that within the next year or two, he would be able to afford one.

Like many Americans, Toby was pleased that these advances in transportation provided more opportunities to enjoy various forms of entertainment. Boxing and baseball were popular spectator sports. Individuals became more active in playing tennis and golf. Vaudeville began in 1883, and the first moving-picture film was shown in 1890. By 1913, vaudeville was a popular form of adult entertainment, and 90 percent of children in the United States had been to the movies.

These changes in entertainment challenged many aspects of traditional life, in particular the concept of nineteenth-century Victorianism and its emphasis on prudish, straight-laced behavior. Many popular movies and vaudeville acts spoofed the Victorian image. Sophie Tucker epitomized this form of entertainment. She began her professional career in burlesque in 1906 and was a star vaudeville performer in 1913. Her act was clearly sexual, as illustrated by one of her songs, "Nobody Loves a Fat Girl, But Oh! How a Fat Girl Can Love." Toby felt guilty laughing at the lyrics of this song because he knew how much his mother was offended by this flippant attack on Victorian values.

Women's roles were also changing. Only a small percentage of Americans attended college in 1913. But of those that did, nearly 40 percent were women. Many states passed women's suffrage laws giving women the right to vote. Women were participating in sports. Tennis and golf were so popular among women that a national tennis championship for women was established in 1887, and the United States Golf Association sponsored the first women's national golf championship in 1895.

More women were working outside the home and were employed in factories, department stores, offices, hospitals, and restaurants. But these women were confronted with many challenges. Toby had just finished reading a report by the Illinois State Vice Committee that said women were often subjected to low wages, poor working conditions, and sexual abuse. Barratt O'Hara, the lieutenant governor of Illinois, was quoted as saying, "There must be something done to protect the young stenographer who is alone in her office all day with her employer."

Toby regarded these changes with mixed feelings. He was raised in a home that took a traditional view on these topics. His mother had taught him, by word and example, the importance of Victorian virtue. She told him that women should not contradict a man's opinion and that it was the duty of men to protect women from worldly experiences. As a result, he was uncomfortable with the explicit sexual content of many vaudeville acts, as well as many of the non-traditional roles women were assuming.

But his friend Bill pointed out the irony of the Victorian Age. He said that while spokesmen of Victorian values taught that women should be placed on a pedestal and protected, prostitution was practiced in cities throughout the United States.

To complicate matters further, Toby fell in love and married someone who could be characterized as a "new woman," a term used to describe a woman who was educated, athletic, socially concerned, and adventurous. In five years of marriage, he had come to understand and appreciate some of Mary's views. He respected his wife's desire to be informed and to have the right to vote. But his traditional views on women still played an important part in his opinions. He believed that women should stay home and take care of their families.

As he arrived home, he decided to stop thinking about social change. It was Friday night, and he was looking forward to a weekend with both Saturday and Sunday free of work responsibilities.

CHAPTER 1

———————————— ▼ ————————————

Detroit's morning sun was warm and bright. A relatively cloudless sky gave every indication that the weather would continue to be extremely hot. It was only nine o' clock, but the temperature was already in the low seventies. The wind, blowing slightly from the southwest, did little to reduce the heat and humidity.

A fat man sat on a pier jutting out into the Detroit River. He hated hot weather. Fortunately, he had found a bench next to a storage shed that provided him with shade. He looked across the river at the Canadian shore, squinting his eyes and resembling a bullfrog in a white linen suit. He waited impatiently for the steamer *Tashmoo* to begin boarding passengers.

He had placed an envelope in the suitcase he had packed the previous evening. Now, after some thought, he decided it would be better to keep the envelope with him. The diamonds in his ring flashed brightly as he leaned over to unbuckle his suitcase. He withdrew the envelope and slipped it into the inside pocket of his suit. He snapped the suitcase shut and walked toward the ship.

The fat man boarded the *Tashmoo* and handed his suitcase to the ship's porter, a young boy with an unusually large nose.

"I'll be getting off in Port Huron, and I want to go directly to Driving Park to watch a few horse races. Please arrange to have my suitcase delivered to the Prince Albert Hotel."

"Yes, sir. That's no problem at all," the porter said.

The fat man nodded, handed the boy a tip, and made his way to C deck. A short man with thinning red hair looked over the edge of his newspaper and watched the fat man find a seat.

*   *   *   *

Mary Sharpe slipped into a tan linen dress that complemented her olive complexion and dark brown eyes. She pulled her long, auburn hair into a loose bun. She reached for her wide-brimmed hat adorned with silk flowers. In doing so, she knocked her husband's hat off the dresser.

She smiled as she retrieved the dark blue patrolman's hat. Her husband, Toby, had just celebrated his first year as a member of the Port Huron Police. Mary knew that Toby's bravery, sensitivity, and open-mindedness would help him become successful; all he lacked was confidence in those abilities. But she knew that as he gained more experience, confidence would come naturally.

Mary walked to the stairs. She could see Toby playing with their two children, four-year-old Chris and two-year-old Amanda. Toby was doing his best to keep both children happy as they played with blocks.

"Mandy!" Chris shouted as he grabbed a block out of Amanda's hand. "I need that to build a fort."

"No!"

Toby took the block from Chris. "She had it first. Maybe you could use this one."

Chris shook his head. "No. It won't look right."

Mary smiled as she watched the living room tableau. Chris sat between his fort and his sister, who, in her ankle-length white dress, looked like an avenging angel. Toby looked a little perplexed. He said, "OK. Let's play with something else."

Mary sat down on the sofa. "What are you planning to do today?"

Toby said, "We're going to South Park this morning. I bought some Oreo cookies to have for lunch with the peach Jell-O you made last night. Then we're going to take very long naps this afternoon."

"Good luck with the naps. You know how much they like to play with their daddy."

Toby feigned a look of despair. "You'll be back early, won't you?"

"We probably won't be back until about four o'clock. After Nancy and I attend the lecture, we're going to the movies. But I promise I won't stop to shop on the way home."

"I forgot about the movie. What are you going to see?"

"Mary Pickford in the *New York Hat*."

"I heard it's really good."

Mary looked at the wall clock. "Well, it's time to go." She nodded at the children. "Make sure they keep their hats on, and don't let them play in this hot sun too long." After a flurry of hugs and kisses, she grabbed her purse and said good-bye.

Mary walked briskly to the trolley stop. She was looking forward to today's speech at the Port Huron Ladies Library Association. Founded in 1866, it was recognized as the second oldest women's club in the United States and ran a library that rented books for a small fee. It also studied current events, particularly women's issues. Today's lecture was going to be after a luncheon at the Harrington Hotel.

She waved to her best friend, Nancy Willard, who was already at the trolley stop.

Nancy said, "This is great. We can ride together."

They paid the nickel fare and sat near the middle of the trolley.

Mary said, "Isn't it exciting that Mrs. Cullenbine was able to stop in Port Huron to talk to us?"

"Yes. A friend of mine heard her talk in Lansing. She said that Mrs. Cullenbine is a compelling speaker."

The two women rode in silence for a few minutes before Nancy said, "Mary, I need to ask you something. Does your husband ever complain about you attending the meetings at the Ladies Library Association?"

"He doesn't say much, but I think he gets a little concerned at times. He certainly doesn't go along with some of the more radical ideas of the suffrage movement. But, he's become more open-mined since we've been married. He even voted yes for women's suffrage in the state referendum last April."

Nancy said, "I wish I could say the same about Elmer. If I just mention Emmeline Pankhurst, Carrie Catt, or any other suffragette, he'll start rolling his eyes. I thought he was going apoplectic when he heard about Margaret Sanger writing those sex education columns for *The Call*."

"Well, I have to admit, Toby had problems with the one she wrote about venereal disease."

Nancy laughed. "That one upset a lot of people. But whenever Elmer says the word feminist, he makes it sound like an obscenity."

"The next time he does that, you should quote Rebecca West."

"Rebecca who?"

Mary said, "She's a young reporter from England. She said that she doesn't know what feminism is, but knows that people call her a feminist whenever she says something that differentiates her from a doormat."

Nancy smiled. "I'll have to remember that."

*   *   *   *

The trolley stopped in front of the Harrington Hotel. The hotel was built in 1896 and had installed a rock spring mineral bath facility in 1908. Mary's father managed a hotel with a mineral bath in Mount Clemens, so she had been around them most of her life. But she never liked them; the smell always reminded her of rotten eggs.

Mary and Nancy entered the lobby, their heels clicking sharply on the marble floor. Nancy was admiring the rich oak paneling when she suddenly stopped and nudged Mary. Nancy nodded her head toward a white-haired man in his sixties, sitting in the far corner. She asked, "Is that him?"

"Who?"

"Thomas Edison. Did you know he stays at the Harrington when he's in town?"

Mary said, "Yes. Toby, my parents, and Bill Boyd told me. It seems like everybody finds it necessary to tell me that Edison lived in Port Huron as a youth and comes back occasionally to visit his family. And when he does, he usually stays here."

"Well, you have only lived here a year. I thought maybe you didn't know. I'm going over to get a better look."

Mary grabbed Nancy's arm. "No, you're not. Leave the man alone. Besides, it's getting late. We need to find a seat for the luncheon."

The white-haired man turned and watched Mary and Nancy disappear into the dining room. He stood up, stuffed some notes about a new invention into his pocket, picked up his cane, and strolled out of the hotel.

CHAPTER 2

▼

Bill Boyd ran as fast as he could toward the ferry. He shouted, "Wait for me!" to the deckhand who was untying the ferry from the dock. Bill was dressed in bright red and blue argyle knee socks and navy blue knickers. With his golf bag in front of him and the socks accenting his skinny legs, he resembled an ostrich.

Only twenty-five years old, Bill Boyd was one of the wealthiest individuals in Port Huron. His father, Abraham Boyd, made a fortune in lumber during the late nineteenth century. In the early 1900s, Abraham founded a newspaper and installed his younger brother as publisher. When Abraham and his wife died, Bill lived with his uncle.

After graduating from Port Huron High School in 1906, Bill attended the University of Michigan, earning a degree in history. Then he went to Europe for a year, spending most of his time in Florence, Italy. Although he enjoyed his year abroad, Bill became increasingly concerned about the militant attitudes in many European countries.

He spent two weeks in Berlin, where he was exposed to a barrage of political speeches reflecting the nationalistic zeal that was sweeping Germany. Kaiser Wilhelm embodied that attitude. His concept of diplomacy was shaking a fist. Bill was glad to return to the United States.

Since his return, he has been employed as a reporter for the *Port Huron Star*. The job gave him considerable satisfaction, but his editorials about the probability of war in Europe did not generate much interest from his readers. He thought it was naïve for the United States to ignore what was happening in Europe.

Bill jumped aboard the ferry and paid his fee. "Whew! I didn't think I was going to make it."

Danny, a young deckhand, said, "We'll always wait for you Mr. Boyd."

Bill gave his golf clubs to Danny and took a seat along the railing. Bill tried to get to Stag Island as often as possible. Stag Island had been a major attraction for the youth in the Port Huron area for the last twenty years. Bill particularly enjoyed playing the nine-hole golf course designed by the Spaulding Sporting Goods Company of Chicago.

Once the ferry was underway, Danny sat beside Bill. "So what are you going to do on Stag Island today?"

Bill said, "The usual. I'm going to play a round of golf and then go fox-trotting at the Griffon Hotel tonight."

"Can you do those new dances?"

"You bet I can. All I need is an attractive, energetic partner."

Danny said, "For a lady-killer like you, I'm sure there won't be any problem finding one. Are you going to do any gambling at the casino?"

"I might try my luck for a while, but I need to get home fairly early."

"Why?"

Bill said, "I'm going to interview a guy from the Michigan State Highway Department in the morning and then take in a baseball game with my old chum in the afternoon."

As the ferry approached Stag Island, Danny stood up to resume working. "You sure are a busy man, Mr. Boyd."

*   *   *   *

Myra Cullenbine, a gaunt, sixty-year-old woman, leaned heavily on her cane as she walked slowly to the podium in the dining room of the Harrington Hotel. For the next hour, her impassioned speech held her audience spellbound. She began by describing the nature of the white slave trade in the United States. She quoted research done by Mr. and Mrs. James Laidlaw of New York City, generally considered the foremost authorities on the subject. She reiterated their claim that about 50,000 girls were kidnapped yearly by ruthless men dubbed Gray Hawks by the press. "Think of that number, ladies—50,000! These unfortunate girls are forced to work in sweatshops, sold as wives, or forced into prostitution.

"The press may refer to the men who capture these innocent women as Gray Hawks, but I think a more appropriate description would be vultures. They must be perceived as the most despicable scavengers in our society.

"Last year, a judge from the Court of General Sessions put John D. Rockefeller Jr. in charge of a grand jury to determine if these charges of white slavery were true. They found that informal networks did in fact exist in New York City. The grand jury indicted more than fifty people, some of whom were policemen.

"And keep this in mind," she continued. "This problem in not confined to large cities like Chicago or New York. According to Edward Petit, immigrant inspector for the U.S. Customs, hundreds of women are smuggled into the United States from Sarnia, Ontario each year. According to Mr. Petit, they are brought across the border in boats or hidden in freight cars that go through the St. Clair River Tunnel.

"We can only conclude that people in Port Huron are assisting in bringing these poor victims into the United States. Some of the girls might even be working in local houses of prostitution.

"We face many dangers in our world today, and the advances we're making in technology may be a contributing factor. Let me make this clear. I am not opposed to cameras, motor cars, or telephones. But for all the good these inventions can bring, there is also the potential for evil. For example, many men are taking photographs of women in nude or compromising positions.

"In conclusion, I believe women can be a major force in correcting many of our country's problems. But in order to do that, we must have the right to vote. Men in your state recently voted down a women's suffrage referendum. But some day, mark my words, some day, *we will have that right!* In the meantime, we need to exert whatever influence we have to promote better government."

As she sat down, the group of women was silent. Then, as one body, they stood up and enthusiastically applauded. Lucy Hendricks, the association president, asked if anyone had any questions.

One woman asked, "Are these women sexually assaulted when they are captured?"

Mrs. Cullenbine said, "It depends on the intention of the captors. If they plan on selling the women as wives, they will not attack them. On the other hand, when the intent is to force the poor victims into prostitution, they will be subjected to repeated sexual assault."

Many women in the audience gasped.

Another woman said, "It's sad that we have all of these problems today. Too bad it's not like the good old days."

Mrs. Cullenbine replied, "I'm not sure how good the good old days were. It was only fifty years ago that our country was torn apart because some people wanted to enslave Africans. That form of slavery involved millions of people, many more than are being affected by the current problem.

"Also, I think problems such as white slavery existed before, but we were not aware of them because newspapers weren't reporting it." She paused for a minute, gazing at the concerned expressions. "It just might be that we are approaching the end of innocence in our country."

Nancy asked, "Hasn't the Mann Act reduced the number of victims of the white slave trade?"

"Yes. Since the Mann Act went into effect in 1910, about a thousand people have been found guilty of taking women across state lines for illegal purposes. But federal resources are stretched very thin."

Mary asked, "Is there anything we can do in Port Huron?"

"That's a good question. I'll tell you what. My train doesn't leave until about four o'clock. I could stay for a few minutes to talk with anyone who is interested in what you might be able to do locally."

Ten women remained. They arranged their chairs in a circle and waited for Myra Cullenbine to begin the impromptu meeting. She said, "The first thing you should do is go to the various law enforcement agencies. You have the local police as well as the Life-Saving Service and the Customs Service. Unfortunately, what you will probably hear is that they do not have the manpower to do more than what they are doing now."

Nancy asked, "What do we do then?"

"One approach is to hire people willing to watch key points of entry. I would guess that one of those would be the St. Clair River Tunnel. It would be fairly easy to monitor the box cars on the trains that stop in Port Huron."

One member of the group asked, "Doesn't the railroad company pay people to do that?"

Mrs. Cullenbine said, "It's true that yard bulls are paid to do that, but they are often paid more money to look the other way. I think it's better to have your own monitors."

"That sounds pretty expensive," Nancy said.

Mrs. Cullenbine looked at her watch. "I am sorry ladies, but I must be leaving. Why don't you take a few minutes to discuss possible solutions. Maybe you can think about some financial resources that might be available."

After Mrs. Cullenbine departed, the women copied down their phone numbers, and discussed individuals and organizations that might give them money. Also, volunteers offered to make appointments to visit the Life-Saving Service, the Customs Service, and the Port Huron police department.

Mary said, "We ought to assume that Myra Cullenbine is right about the law enforcement agencies. Is it all right that if anyone can get people to volunteer to watch the tunnel, they should go ahead and do it?"

Nancy said, "That sounds like a good idea to me." Several women nodded in agreement.

"OK," Mary said. "Let's plan on meeting next Saturday. How about meeting here at noon for lunch?"

Mary and Nancy left the meeting in a somber mood. Mary said, "I don't feel like going to the movies today."

Nancy nodded. "Me either. I just want to go home and hug my babies."

*   *   *   *

Mary returned home to see Toby sprawled on the floor, sleeping. As she walked over to kiss him, he opened his eyes. He picked up his copy of *Riders of the Purple Sage*. "I was looking forward to reading more about how Zane Grey described the Mormon practice of polygamy, but I fell asleep about five minutes after I put the children down for their naps."

Mary asked, "How did things go?"

"Fine. It was a lot of fun, but it sure was tiring." Toby glanced at the clock. "It's only three o'clock. Did you walk out of the movie?"

"We didn't go. We weren't in the mood to watch Mary Pickford being romanced after what we heard today."

"What do you mean?"

"Mrs. Cullenbine spent most of the time talking about white slavery. She claims that hundreds of women are smuggled into the United States through our city every year."

"Here in Port Huron? Are you sure?"

Mary said, "She quoted an immigration inspector by the name of Edward Petit who claims it's true. After the talk, a group of women met to see what could be done to stop it."

"Let me guess. You and Nancy were two of those women."

"Yes, I was. So was Sylvia Pointe, the secretary from the police department. She'll probably tell you all about it Monday."

Toby rolled his eyes. "Oh, you can count on that. What did you come up with?"

"One possibility would be to monitor the St. Clair River Tunnel. We're going to talk to various government authorities next week. Also, I thought Bill Boyd might be interested in hiring some people to watch the tunnel."

"Are you sure you want to do that? It might put Bill and the people he hires at risk. Plus, I think it's too dangerous for women to get involved in something like that."

Mary said, "We're not going to do anything reckless. But we need to do something to protect these women. It's like Jane Withersteen in the book you're reading, when she's being pressured to marry someone who already had a wife." She took the book from Toby and flipped through the pages. "Darn, I can't find the passage. But when you read it, you'll see that Jane Withersteen says something like, 'freedom is the right of all women'." She handed the book back to Toby. "We need to do what we can to give these women who are being kidnapped that same right."

Toby studied the determined look on Mary's face. "Bill's dropping by tomorrow to pick me up for the ball game. Maybe you can talk to him then." He reached over and held her hands. "I know this is important to you, but please be careful. If white slavery is going on in Port Huron, the people involved are dangerous and won't stop at anything if someone gets in their way."

CHAPTER 3

▼

The Winslow Shirt Company was located near downtown Toronto. The brick structure, with rows of small windows, resembled a prison. The interior did little to change that impression. Women, mostly immigrants, worked for ten hours a day, Monday through Friday. A foreman, convincingly playing the role of prison guard, paced the floor.

The workers doing the jobs that required the most skill huddled in front of sewing machines, carefully stitching shirts together. Because of the intricate nature of their job, management reluctantly provided them with a well-lit area. The other women sat in semi-darkness, doing mindless, repetitive jobs like cutting patterns, attaching buttons, and packaging the completed product. Regardless of their job, all the women were sweltering in the intense summer heat. Three women collapsed the day before and had to be carried outside.

The women were given a wonderful treat on Saturdays: they only had to work eight hours. The older women, numbed by the boring routine, were grateful for two fewer hours of work. They sat at their stations and stared morosely at the clock as it neared five.

To the young, single women, the end of Saturday's workday meant something different. Their stamina had not yet been drained. It was Saturday night! They would be able to sleep late tomorrow. And maybe, just maybe, a better job might be available next week. They were still young enough to dream of a brighter future.

Soma Fekete and Zizi Balogh talked excitedly as they walked out the factory door. They were in their early twenties and had lived in Toronto for less than a year. The working conditions at the shirt factory were no worse than what they experienced in Hungary, and the pay was better. Immigrating to Canada was a dream come true.

Zizi asked, "Where do you want to go tonight?"

Soma swung her purse enthusiastically. "I want to go dancing at the Imperial Ball Room."

"Do you think Nikki will be there?"

Soma said, "I hope so."

Zizi lifted her dress to her knees and began swaying her hips. "Oh, Nikki. Let us do one more dance."

Soma laughed and gave Zizi a friendly shove. "Stop that. You know that I am not that kind of girl."

"Do you think Nikki is serious about you?"

"I believe he might be. He was asking me many personal questions last week. I would like him to be serious about me."

Zizi took Soma's hand. "Then we must make you beautiful for tonight. It is time to remember the old Hungarian proverb—'Adam ate the apple, and our teeth still ache.' When Nikki sees you tonight, all of his teeth will ache."

They skipped down the street, holding hands and singing. They entered the alley that they used as a shortcut to their apartment. When they were halfway through the alley, a horse-drawn carriage blocked the exit. A small man in laborer's clothes stepped down. He took off his cap and waved to Soma and Zizi. He said, "Excuse me. I'm lost. Could you give me directions?"

Soma said, "We will try to help."

When the women approached the carriage, the man drew a knife. He said, "What I really want is for you to get into the carriage."

The women turned to run back the way they had come. But a huge man blocked their way.

Grabbing Zizi by the arm, the small man whispered, "Don't yell for help and you won't get hurt."

Soma asked, "What are you going to do with us?"

He smiled. "We'll talk about that later."

The small man pushed the women inside, jumped up on the carriage, and flicked the reins lightly. Inside, the terrified women sat staring at the menacing eyes of the other kidnapper.

*   *   *   *

Detective John Gressley of the Port Huron police department closed the door to his Erie Street apartment and walked south toward the Black River. He had spent eight hours at the police station, mostly doing paperwork, and needed some light entertainment. The vaudeville presentation at the Majestic Theater promised to satisfy his need. Tonight's show was entitled *Henpecked Henry* and featured Halton Powell.

Since the sun was still shining brightly, Gressley tried to stay in the shade as much as possible. He hoped his new Winslow shirt would not be saturated with perspiration by the time he got to the theater. Gressley approached Port Huron High School. Opened in 1908, the three-story building was nearly a block long. A previous high school, built at the same site, had been constructed in 1870. A fire destroyed it in 1906. Toby Sharpe and Bill Boyd were in the last senior class at the old building.

Forty-four students graduated from Port Huron High School this year. They celebrated with a banquet at the Harrington Hotel. On graduation night, they listened to a commencement speech entitled "Is Public School a Failure?" Gressley never found out if the answer was yes or no. He wondered how receptive the graduates were to even hearing the question. He was told that Percival Jones, the father of one of the graduates, began snoring during the speech.

Gressley walked past the high school, turned unto Butler Street, and headed toward his destination. The Majestic Theater, built by the O'Neill brothers, opened in 1906. It had a capacity of 1,500, with the number of seats being divided nearly equally between parquet, balcony, and gallery.

A few famous entertainers, including Sara Bernhardt and the great Scottish singer Harry Lauder, appeared at the Majestic. Gressley remembered how the audience applauded Lauder when he sang songs like "There's a Wee Hoose Mang the Heather," and "Just a Wee Deoch an Doris."

Gressley entered the theater and was walking toward his seat when he heard a familiar voice.

"Detective Gressley. Fancy meeting you here." He saw Sylvia Pointe, a secretary at the police department, smiling at him.

"Hello Sylvia. Are you here to acquire some culture?"

"I'm not sure how cultured tonight's performance will be, but it sounds like fun."

"You mean to tell me that you're not overly impressed by the potential of a show called *Henpecked Henry?*"

Sylvia said, "Should I be? Are you meeting anyone?"

"No. Would you like to sit together?"

"That would be nice."

They walked to the parquet section. After they were seated, Gressley asked, "Did you attend today's speech at the Ladies Library Association?"

"Yes. Mrs. Cullenbine was impressive. A few of us met afterwards to see what might be done to keep Port Huron from being involved in white slave trade."

"Like what?"

Sylvia said, "One suggestion was to post guards at the St. Clair River Tunnel. Mrs. Cullenbine thought that it might be one of the places where women are smuggled into the United States."

"I can tell you right now that the police department won't be able to help. Our budget is stretched too thin already."

The lights dimmed. Sylvia said, "Maybe we can talk about it after the show." Halton Powell, the star of *Henpecked Henry*, shambled on stage. Sylvia placed her hand on Gressley's knee. He discreetly covered her hand with his hat.

*   *   *   *

A canopy of bright stars glittered in the cloudless summer sky as a solitary figure rowed along the Lake Huron shore. The boat paused for a moment and then headed toward the sandy beach.

A fat man stood on the beach, his beefy arms folded across his large stomach. He said, "You brought me out here in the middle of the night and then show up in a stupid rowboat?"

"I had to try one more time to get you to reconsider. Besides, you're the one who said we shouldn't be seen together."

The fat man refused to help pull the boat ashore. He said, "You're going to have to be very persuasive if you expect me to change my mind."

The conversation soon increased in volume as the two voices were raised in anger. Finally, the fat man gave a dismissive wave and walked toward a wooded lot. He did not pay attention to the steps behind him. Nor did he see a blade protruding from a gloved fist. But he felt a sharp pain when the blade was plunged into his back.

He screamed and flailed his arms in an attempt to protect himself. But the strength of the blow forced him to his knees. The assailant withdrew the blade and repeatedly swung it viciously across the victim's neck and back. When the violent attack stopped, the fat man was dead.

A short distance away, a light appeared in a window of the Fort Gratiot Lighthouse. The murderer remained still until the light went off. With effort, the murderer rolled the corpse into the wooded lot and covered it with underbrush. A wallet and envelope were removed from the dead man's suit jacket. The murderer ran to the shore, jumped into the boat, and began rowing. When the boat was away from the shore the murderer threw the wallet into the lake before continuing. The envelope remained on the seat of the rowboat.

In the distance, a revolving beam of light from the Fort Gratiot Lighthouse skimmed across the cool, dark, blue water of Lake Huron.

CHAPTER 4

▼

Soma and Zizi lay bound and gagged in the living room of an abandoned house in the outskirts of Toronto. They had spent the night wondering why they were there. Two men had forced them into a carriage but never attempted to molest them. Nor did they give any reason for their abduction.

Fear—of the unknown, of the men, of what would happen to them, of losing their jobs—overwhelmed them. Their only solace was prayer. Both women flinched when the door opened. One of the kidnappers, a small man named Charlie had a face that reminded one of a hawk.

"Thought you might want some breakfast." He set two bowls down and squatted to remove the gags and ropes.

"I'm keeping your feet tied, so don't get any ideas about runnin' away."

Zizi asked, "Why are we here?"

"Now you don't worry about that. Just eat your Post Toasties."

Zizi began eating immediately. Soma pushed her bowl away. She said, "Our families will miss us."

"You wouldn't try to put one over on ol' Charlie, would you? We know you came to Canada without your families. Just a couple of attractive women alone in a new country, looking for something better. Well, we're going to make your dreams come true."

Zizi asked, "What do you mean?"

"You're staying here for a couple of days. Then we'll take a little train ride to the good old U.S. of A."

Soma said, "We do not want to go to the United States. We want to stay in Canada!"

"Sorry, honey," he said. "You don't have a choice."

A burly man with a bushy mustache entered the room. He said, "So our juicy foreign dishes made it through the night, huh?" He grabbed Zizi's hair and pulled her head back.

Charlie said, "Leave her alone, Carl."

"Come on. We're going to be here for a couple of days. We ought to have some fun."

"You know that's not the deal."

Carl stared angrily at Charlie. He let go of Zizi's hair with a jerk and stomped out the room.

Soma pleaded with Charlie. "Please tell us what you are going to do to us."

"You'll know soon enough." He gently rubbed Soma's shoulder. "It will do you some good if you ate your cereal."

Soma picked up a spoon and slowly began to eat.

When the women finished eating, Charlie retied their hands and left the room. Zizi and Soma sat looking at each other, confused and afraid.

*   *   *   *

Bill Boyd entered the Hotel Marion and walked purposefully to the front desk.

"I have an appointment to interview Edgar Reynolds of the Michigan State Highway Department. Is he still in his room?"

The desk clerk pointed toward the dining room. "He went in there a few minutes ago. He's the short, red-haired man sitting in the corner near the windows."

Edgar Reynolds stood up as Bill approached his table. Bill's hearty handshake was abandoned when he felt Reynolds' soft, limp hand. *Holy Toledo*, Bill thought. *It feels like I'm shaking hands with a wet dishcloth.* He said, "Mr. Reynolds, thank you for agreeing to be interviewed this morning."

"Good morning Mr. Boyd. I'm honored to be asked. I went ahead and obtained a table since it was so busy in the dining room this morning." Bill noticed that Reynolds' voice had an unmistakable professorial tone.

"Yes, the Hotel Marion is popular. Many of the diners arrived on the *Tashmoo* to spend the weekend in Port Huron."

Reynolds peered over his reading glasses. "I can see why it's popular. The architecture is impressive. It's characteristic of the organic style of Louis Sullivan and Frank Lloyd Wright. They're two of the most influential architects of our time."

Good Lord, Bill thought. *This sounds like* it's *going to be a boring interview.* He said, "I'm familiar with their influence."

"I'm sorry. I didn't mean to insult you."

Bill laughed. "That's OK. But you should realize that just because some of our residents refer to our city as 'Por Churn,' many of us are aware of what goes on in the world."

Reynolds offered a thin smile. "Point taken. I guess we both know about Wright's architecture."

Before they could continue, a waiter appeared at the table. Bill ordered bacon, eggs, potatoes, toast, and coffee. Reynolds ordered only toast with orange marmalade and coffee. He patted his stomach. "I'm trying to lose a few pounds."

After the waiter left, Reynolds said, "I have a question about another local building. What is the one about a block from here that looks like a castle?"

"Oh, that's the Maccabees Temple. The Knights of the Maccabees built their first temple on that site about twenty years ago. They expanded it in 1900 and named it the Second Maccabees Temple."

"Who are the Knights of the Maccabees?"

Bill said, "It's a fraternal organization that provides insurance for its members. It has a woman's auxiliary called the Ladies of the Maccabees of the World, who now occupy that building. The Ladies of the Maccabees is the largest fraternal beneficiary order of women in the world."

"I couldn't help but notice the odd-looking copper domes on the building's roof. They look like spaceships from H. G. Wells' *War of the Worlds.*"

"They're called hives."

Reynolds looked puzzled. "What do you mean, 'hives?'"

"They are Macca-beehives."

"Are you kidding me?"

Bill laughed. "No. I don't know exactly what it means, but I do know that the Ladies of the Maccabees are organized into chapters called hives. In fact, Port Huron Hive Number One has about four hundred members."

Reynolds shook his head. "We certainly live in interesting times."

The waiter returned with their meals. Bill picked up his fork. Before he began eating, he said, "Thanks again for taking time to be interviewed."

"You're welcome. Where do you want to start?"

"I understand you joined the Michigan State Highway Department shortly after its creation in 1905. Why were you interested in that area?"

"I could see the need for better roads several years ago when the bicyclists formed the League of American Wheelmen and wanted improvements. They began to exert political influence when a coalition of bicyclists and other interest groups combined to create the Good Roads Movement. Do you know that Horatio Earle, our current Michigan state highway commissioner, was one of its leaders?"

Bill scribbled down the information. He said, "No. I didn't know that."

"Indeed he was. He also facilitated the first International Good Roads Conference in 1900 and then was appointed Michigan's highway commissioner in 1905."

"Several groups opposed the Good Roads Movement when it first began. Why was that?"

Reynolds replied, "Farmers were probably the most vocal in their opposition. They believed bicyclists were a nuisance and that the taxes would be too high."

"Aren't farmers in favor of improved roads now?"

Reynolds nodded. "Rather ironic, isn't it? I think the emerging importance of motor vehicles is a major reason. Many farmers now realize that the current road system is totally inadequate for their future needs."

Bill said, "As a car owner, I find the construction of paved roads to be too slow. When the first mile of concrete road in the country was built near Detroit, I had great hopes. But now it's four years later, and there are fewer than 500 miles of concrete roads in the entire country."

"That's true. But I'm sure the construction will be faster as more people buy cars and especially now that the farmers support the idea."

Bill said, "Let's talk about this year. This is proving to be a pivotal year for many counties in Michigan, isn't it? Only about half of the counties had road commissions at the beginning of the year. Now, the voters in many counties gave their approval."

"Yes. The method used by the state in collecting and distributing taxes played an important part."

"Why is that?"

"Michigan collected taxes from all the counties but only gave money to the ones that had county road commissions."

Bill grinned, "I guess that would encourage people to vote yes. What happens now that the voters in St. Clair County gave their approval in the April election?"

"First, the elected commissioners had to meet and select a chairman. They did that in June when they chose Charles Bailey. Then they had to recommend a road system."

"When will they do that?"

"They already have."

"No kidding. I never heard of government moving so fast."

Reynolds withdrew a document from his jacket and placed it in front of Bill. "Here it is. They are proposing three trunk lines and four county roads. I think it's a good plan."

Bill looked at the document for a few minutes. "What's the difference between a trunk line and a county road?"

"The trunk lines will someday be part of the state system and will be rewarded with twice as much money as the county roads."

Bill said, "With all the thousands of miles that will be paved, that's going to cost a lot of money. I imagine some people are going to get rich."

"That might include a company right here in your city. The Port Huron Engine and Thresher Company manufactures road rollers and scarifiers."

"Scarifiers?"

"They are machines with big claws that will break up the soil so we can smooth it out to lay the road."

"With all of that money, is the state concerned about graft?"

"There are always unscrupulous businessmen who will try to get an advantage. The state and local governments are going to have to be vigilant to make sure the money is used properly."

"That brings us to your current visit to Port Huron. What are your plans for the next two days?"

Reynolds said, "I'll meet with county road commissions and other county officials in order to help coordinate things. I'll be meeting with representatives of St. Clair and Lapeer Counties tomorrow. On Tuesday, representatives from the remaining Thumb counties—Sanilac, Huron, and Tuscola—will be in town."

"What will you talk about?"

"We'll discuss the financial aspect of road building in the mornings and spend the afternoons talking about construction plans."

Bill asked, "Will I be able to attend?"

"Certainly. These meetings are open to the public. We're going to be meeting in the Blue Room, just down the main hallway."

Bill closed his notebook. "Thanks for the interview. It's been very informative."

Reynolds nodded politely. "Now I have some questions for you. What does one do in Port Huron on a Sunday afternoon?"

Bill thought it was time to promote Port Huron.

The waiter returned to refill their coffee and remove the dirty dishes. He asked if they would like anything else. Both men declined.

After the waiter left, Bill said, "There's plenty going on today. If you like baseball, Port Huron's professional team is playing at Athletic Field. Their star pitcher, Louis Corbat, is scheduled to be on the mound. If you fancy horse racing, you can go to Driving Park."

Reynolds wrinkled his nose. "I'm not exactly interested in sports."

Bill thought for a moment. "Well, I think a community band is going to be playing at the pavilion at Pine Grove Park. They start playing at one o'clock and will be featuring Sousa marches."

"That sounds fine. How do I get there?"

"Just catch the city trolley outside the hotel. The park is about five or six blocks from here."

Reynolds asked, "Is Pine Grove Park scenic? I'm interested in taking some photographs while I'm here."

"Then you should enjoy your visit. The park is attractive and it's right on the beautiful St. Clair River."

Reynolds' eyes brightened. "That sounds wonderful. Being a government employee is my profession, but photography is my passion."

The two men stood. "Thanks for the suggestions," Reynolds said. "Now, if you don't mind, I have some paperwork that needs to be completed for tomorrow."

"Of course." Bill held out his hand, expecting another limp handshake. He was not disappointed.

CHAPTER 5

▼

Bill peered through the screen door. "Is anyone home?"

Mary opened the door and smiled. "Bill, can you come in for a few minutes? I have something I want to talk to you about."

Bill sprawled on the sofa. "Sure. Where's the rest of your family?"

"They're outside for a few minutes. Toby thought it would be better if we were alone."

"By Jove, this sounds serious."

"It is. Do you know anything about white slavery?"

He held up his hands. "Not personally." He saw the grim look on Mary's face and decided this was not a good time to joke around. "I read the Associated Press article we published in the paper last week. That's about all I know about it."

"Mrs. Cullenbine talked about it yesterday at the Ladies Library Association lecture. She said that it's very possible that women are being smuggled into Port Huron from Canada."

"Isn't that a job for the federal government?"

"We're going to talk to them this week, but they're likely to say they have too much to do already."

"So what do you want me to do, write an article in the paper?"

Mary hesitated, reluctant to ask for money. She decided to be blunt. "I was wondering if you would be able to hire some men to monitor the St. Clair River Tunnel for a while."

Bill sat up straight. "My, that is an interesting idea."

"Young women are apparently put in boxcars and transported into the United States."

"Good Lord. Are you suggesting that if we watched the freight trains that stop in Port Huron, we might actually see smuggling take place?"

"That's what I had in mind."

"What would we do if we saw that happen? We wouldn't have any authority to detain them."

Mary said, "You could follow them to see where they go. Then you could call the police or write an article in the newspaper about what you saw."

Bill stood up. "By George, that sounds exciting! Maybe I could do something that would rival Upton Sinclair's *The Jungle*. Let me think about it and get back to you later."

*   *   *   *

An attractive, young woman crossed Pine Grove Avenue and entered Pine Grove Park. Charla, tall and well-proportioned, wore a light blue dress that highlighted her dark blue eyes. Her shoulder-length black hair swayed slightly as she walked toward the pavilion. If she was aware of the admiring glances, she did not show it. She closed her parasol and sat in the last row of seats.

Despite the stirring renditions of Sousa's marches, Charla began to feel restless and was about to leave when a man seated several rows in front of her removed his boater to wipe his forehead. Suddenly, Charla snapped to attention. *It's him! It's that creep, Reynolds.* Charla had not seen him for seven years. His red hair was thinner, and he had added some weight. But she was sure it was him. She stood up to see if she could get a better look. She saw the camera resting on his lap. Feeling nauseated, she sat down.

Looking around, she noticed two young teenage boys taking turns throwing a pocketknife at a target pinned to a tree. They wore their knickerbockers below their knees and their caps backward. Charla thought they were the type of youngsters that could help her out.

She walked over to the boys and said, "Hi. I've been admiring your skill. You're really good at that. By the way, my name is Charla."

The younger boy did not respond. But the older boy, admiring Charla's well-formed body, nodded his head. He said, "Hi. I'm Luke Laboy, and this is my younger brother Mark."

Charla smiled. "Would you be interested in doing me a favor? I'll make it worth your while."

Mark threw his knife at the target, hitting the middle. Luke said, "Good shot." Turning to Charla, he said, "Sure, we don't have anything else to do. What you got in mind?"

Charla pointed toward the bandstand. "I want you to play a practical joke on the red-haired man sitting in the second row." She leaned forward and explained her idea. She concluded by giving Luke a slip of paper and each of the boys a dollar. "When you're done, come to this address, and I'll give both of you two more dollars."

Luke said, "Yes, ma'am!"

Mark took off immediately in the direction of the St. Clair River, while Charla left the park in the opposite direction. Luke turned his cap around and lowered its bill over his eyes. He leaned against a tree and cleaned his fingernails with his pocketknife as he watched Reynolds.

After the band concert, Reynolds walked over to the river. He sat on a park bench and observed the various boats moving up and down the St. Clair River. Every type of craft imaginable seemed to be plying the river's blue waters. There were rowboats filled with fishermen. He also saw freighters, sailboats, and tugboats.

Reynolds turned his attention to a group of teenagers swimming in the rapid currents. As he was watching, two of the girls got out of the river and walked in Reynolds's direction. They removed their bathing caps and sat on the grass a few feet in front of Reynolds. The wet swimsuits clung to their bodies, highlighting their attractive shapes.

Reynolds tipped his hat in their direction. "Good afternoon, girls. Isn't that river a bit dangerous for swimming?"

Beth said, "Yes, but we're real careful. We don't go out very far."

After a brief conversation, Reynolds picked up his camera. "Is it OK if I take your pictures?"

Helen giggled. "Maybe." The girls smiled shyly as Reynolds took several shots.

Reynolds said. "Do you think there's someplace we could meet later? I could get better lighting, and the pictures would look nicer."

"Golly Molly, I don't know about that mister."

Reynolds was about to speak again when suddenly Mark ran by and threw a pail of water on him. Reynolds jumped up and ran after Mark. After running for several yards, he realized he would not be able to catch the fleet-footed youngster. He shook his fist. "Confound you!" Breathing heavily, he turned back to the girls, but they were gone.

Disgusted, Reynolds walked through the park to catch the trolley to return to the Hotel Marion. He asked the front desk if there were any messages for him.

The desk clerk said, "Yes sir. You have one letter."

Reynolds took the letter and walked up the stairs to his room. He had not noticed a young boy get off the trolley and follow him up the stairs.

Twenty minutes later, Luke and Mark went to a boardinghouse on Lincoln Avenue. Charla was waiting on the front porch. She directed them toward the corner, several feet from the boardinghouse. She said, "Did you get the information?"

Luke said, "He's in room 210 of the Hotel Marion."

Charla gave the boys the promised money. She said, "Thanks. I really appreciate your help today."

Mark gushed, "It was fun."

Charla smiled as she watched the two boys strut down the street. "Luke," she called. "Will you come back for a minute?"

Luke ran back and asked what she wanted.

"I could use your help tomorrow. Do you think you could meet me at the Prince Albert Hotel at eight o'clock in the morning?"

"You bet. Do you want Mark to come along?"

"No," Charla said. This is a one-person job, and I think you're the one I can trust to do it. In fact, make sure you don't tell anybody else about it, including Mark."

"Whatever you say, Charla. I won't let you down. See you tomorrow at eight." Luke ran to catch up with Mark, as the two of them entered Pine Grove Park. They bought four Coca-Colas at the concession stand and carried them to where Beth and Helen were sitting.

Mark handed Beth a Coke and plopped down beside her. He said, "Can you believe it? That lady gave Luke and me three dollars each."

Helen said, "That's wonderful. You should have seen that man's face turn red when you threw the water on him."

Beth said, "That was fun, but we better be careful. That woman might get us into trouble."

Mark said, "I doubt if we'll ever see her again."

Luke smiled and took a long drink.

CHAPTER 6

▼

Louis Corbat stood motionless on the pitcher's mound as he received signs from the catcher. Then he began his windup. Seconds later, the game ended as the pop fly nestled securely in the second baseman's glove. The sparse but enthusiastic crowd was immediately on its feet, cheering.

"Holy smokes!" yelled Toby. "He actually threw a no-hitter."

"That young pitcher deserves a reward!" Bill removed his hat and began circulating among the spectators. "Give a bonus to Corbat; put some money in the hat." People threw various coins into the makeshift collection plate. "Hey, we can do better than that," he chided. He then ceremoniously placed three dollars in his hat.

"No wonder the newspaper costs so much, if a second-rate reporter like you has that much money to throw around," someone yelled good-naturedly. But Bill's generosity encouraged larger donations. As Toby waited, Bill called Corbat over to the bleachers. Bill said, "On behalf of the fans who witnessed a masterful pitching performance, I want to present you with nearly fifty dollars."

The youthful pitcher blushed as Bill presented him with the money and posed for a photo for the *Port Huron Star*. Corbat said, "Gee thanks. Maybe I should pitch no-hitters more often."

Bill said, "Pitch more games like this, and you'll be pitching in a Class C league soon. Now go celebrate with your teammates."

Toby walked down the bleachers to where Bill was standing. After watching Corbat's teammates carry him off the field on their shoulders, the two friends left Athletic Park.

Toby Sharpe and Bill Boyd began their friendship at age ten when they played baseball together. Sharpe's stocky figure and fearless attitude made him a successful catcher. On the other hand, Bill was usually positioned where he would be less likely to be confronted with a fly ball. A few years later, Toby was the star catcher on Port Huron High's team. Bill was student manager until he got kicked off the team for arguing with the coach. Now in their mid-twenties, they had maintained an interest in baseball and were happy that a minor league team was in Port Huron. The Class D Border League was the lowest level of professional ball and games were played only on weekends. Still, the games were fun to watch. But Bill and Toby knew that if attendance didn't pick up, there would not be a team next year.

"That three-dollar donation was impressive," said Toby.

Bill gave a wry smile. "Well, I can afford three dollars more than most of those fans can afford a quarter."

Toby smiled. "You're a good egg, Bill Boyd."

They seated themselves in Bill's two-passenger Havers speedster. The car was bright red with custom-made chrome trim. The seats were upholstered in brown leather. Toby was always teasing Bill about his expensive motor car, saying he should get a good cheap car like the Ford Model T. Bill would just grin and explain that he liked the idea of buying a car that was built in Port Huron. He figured that if he had any problems, he could go right to the factory.

Bill pulled smoothly out of the parking lot onto Seventh Street. He asked if Toby wanted to go right home.

"Yeah. I promised Mary we would take the kids for a walk before supper. Have you been over to Stag Island yet this summer?"

"As a matter of fact, I was there yesterday. I played a little golf in the afternoon and then went dancing at the Griffon Hotel."

"Did you take Irene?"

Bill said, "Didn't I tell you? We broke up about a month ago. But I did meet a beautiful redhead firecracker from Marine City—Maggie McGinnity."

Bill's love life always fascinated Toby. Bill would fall head over heels for someone who seemed to be an extrovert like Bill. After a short, frantic relationship, they would break up. Toby thought the problem was that the women were too much like Bill.

Bill asked, "How's Mary?"

"Fine."

"If I ever settle down and get married, I hope I'm lucky enough to find someone like her. But what is this thing about monitoring the tunnel for kidnappers?"

Toby shrugged his shoulders. "She went to a talk at the Ladies Library Association yesterday, and now she wants to protect Port Huron from the white slave trade."

"She sounds like a good example of the 'new woman.'"

"Is that the term I've been reading about in the newspaper?"

Bill said, "Yes. It's what newspapers are now calling women who are breaking away from the old-fashioned Victorian image. They are intelligent, open to new ideas, and willing to be involved in social activities."

"That's Mary. She was active during the women's suffrage vote in April. But I think this white slavery issue is going a little too far."

"Why?"

Toby said, "I just think that the main responsibility for a woman is her family. When women get too involved in other things, it's not good for society."

Bill laughed. "You sound like the same old Toby."

"What do you mean?"

"Remember when you gave that speech in English class on why women should not have the right to vote?"

Toby groaned. "Good Lord, don't remind me of that! Half of the girls wouldn't talk to me for a month. But I changed my mind on that topic."

Bill said, "And if you keep an open mind, who knows what you'll start believing."

*   *   *   *

Albert Fleming put down the newspaper and removed his reading glasses. "Why don't you sit down, Mildred? You're going to wear the carpet out."

Mildred walked to the living room window of their boardinghouse and looked down the street for what seemed the hundredth time. "I'm sorry Albert, but I just can't help worrying about those two girls. They should have come home from work yesterday."

Albert stood up and walked over to his wife. He spoke gently, "They'll be home soon. They probably went to a party and stayed at someone's house for the night."

Mildred wiped a tear from her cheek. "Maybe Zizi would do something like that but not Soma. I think something terrible has happened to them."

Albert patted his wife's shoulder. "You care deeply for those girls, don't you?"

Mildred nodded, "They've brought so much energy to our house. It's been such a joy to see how they have met the challenges of moving to a new country. I would feel terrible if something bad happened to them."

Albert took Mildred's hand and led her to the sofa. "Let's wait one more day. If they don't return tonight, we'll go to the police tomorrow."

*   *   *   *

Mary Sharpe sat on the sofa in her home, reading Edith Wharton's *Ethan Frome*. This was her favorite book, and she was about halfway through a second reading. Her children were still napping and Toby had yet to return from the baseball game. She always found these rare moments of solitude refreshing.

Mary and Toby met while working in Mount Clemens. Mary's father was a manager for the Macomb County Bath Company, owners of the Alexandria Hotel. Thousands of people from around the country would come to the Alexandria Hotel to soak in the highly salted mineral waters. The bathers believed that the repulsive-smelling water would cure anything from eczema to insomnia, from alcoholism to rheumatism.

Mary worked at the front desk, while Toby had a variety of jobs. Mary teased Toby about his so-called jobs, because the main reason for his employment was to be on the semi-pro baseball team sponsored by the Bath Company. He was paid twice as much as other employees, but spent most of his time playing baseball. Toby had been offered a professional contract, but he didn't like the idea of moving from one city to another all the time. He might have become a professional if he thought he could have made it to the majors. But he knew that his inability to hit curve balls consistently would relegate him to the lower levels of professional baseball.

Shortly after they were married, it became obvious that Toby needed a job with a future. When a job with the Port Huron Police became available, both agreed it was time to leave Mount Clemens.

Mary missed her family occasionally. But Mount Clemens was only an hour ride on the Grand Trunk Railroad, so they were able to see each other fairly often. In fact, her parents and younger sister were planning to come to Port Huron in about a month to participate in the Chautauqua week at Pine Grove Park. The Port Huron Men's Association was organizing an entire week of lectures, music, and plays patterned after the famous resort in Chautauqua, New York. Mary was especially looking forward to the performance of Shakespeare's *Comedy of Errors*.

Her quiet interlude was abruptly ended when the phone began ringing. As Mary walked to the phone, she reflected on how grateful she was for the development of the wall phone in 1907. It was more convenient and much more attractive than its predecessors. She stood in front of the large, two-foot-long wooden box on the wall. Since she was barely five feet tall, she had to adjust the mouthpiece to accommodate her diminutive stature. She removed the receiver from its cradle. "Hello."

"Hi, Mary."

"Oh mother, I'm glad you called."

"I'm calling to see if you have everything arranged for our visit."

Mary said, "Yes. I reserved a room for you and Dad at the Harrington Hotel for the week. Does Rebecca still want to stay with us?"

"Good heavens, yes. She can't wait to play with her niece and nephew."

Mary said, "I bought week passes for Chautauqua. Do you know we get to see twenty-one events for only two dollars?"

"My, that's certainly reasonable. Your father and I are looking forward to our visit. Kiss my grandchildren for me."

"I will. They can hardly wait to see you. Good-bye for now."

Mary hung up and returned to the sofa. She was about to sit down when the phone rang again.

Toby jumped out of Bill's car, thanked him for the ride, and walked briskly up the sidewalk. His two children would be waking up from their naps, and he knew Mary would be waiting, eager to have a Sunday stroll.

She was waiting but not with the look Toby expected. She said, "Detective Gressley just called. They found a body near the Fort Gratiot Lighthouse."

*   *   *   *

As Patrolman Sharpe approached the lighthouse, he could see the tall, slender figure of Detective John Gressley talking to a number of people who had gathered on the beach. Gressley was wearing a three-piece herringbone tweed suit with a starched wing-collar shirt. For a hat, he wore a stylish summer boater.

Ever since Toby joined the police department last year, Gressley always intimidated him. As detective, Gressley was the third-highest ranking member of the department. Above him were Chief George Chambers and Captain Richard Kerwin. There had been some discussion about creating the rank of lieutenant but no action had been taken.

Toby's feeling of intimidation usually led to a degree of awkwardness when he had to address the detective. Was he Mr. Gressley, or detective? Toby would never consider calling him John. Rather than trying to figure out which Gressley preferred, he resorted to "sir."

Gressley thanked the people and walked over to Toby. He puffed deeply on a cigarette, frowned, and said, "Nice to see you could make it, Patrolman Sharpe."

"I came as soon as I could, sir."

Gressley offered a slight nod and led Toby to a clump of trees. "A man found the body about an hour ago. His dog ran into that wooded area and started sniffing around. When the man caught up with the dog, he could see a body hidden beneath some underbrush."

Gagging slightly, Toby positioned himself so that he would not have to look too closely at the corpse. Toby asked, "Who is he?"

"So far, no one has recognized him. How about you?"

"No. I don't think I ever saw him before."

"Then why don't you tell me what your impressions are of the crime scene."

Toby shot Gressley a quick glance and wondered if it was some kind of test. He looked at the terrible wounds on the back and neck. "Well, he appears to have been murdered."

"That's good," said Gressley, trying to suppress a grin. "Anything else?"

"The fancy diamond ring and his clothes suggest he was pretty rich. Was his wallet missing?"

"Yes."

"So the motive could have been robbery."

Gressley asked, "Then why not take that expensive ring?"

"Maybe the killer didn't have time, or perhaps he couldn't get it off the man's chubby finger. Was he murdered in the woods?"

Gressley pointed to a spot on the beach. He said, "He was killed over there. That dark area in the sand is blood. He was rolled into the woods."

"What about footprints?"

"A lot of people walk along here, so it would be impossible to tell which ones would belong to the killer. There were some indentations in the sand that the murderer might have made when pushing the body. But I'm afraid they wouldn't help identify anyone."

Toby asked, "When was he killed?"

"Sometime around midnight."

"Why would he come out here in the middle of the night?"

Gressley said, "Greed and sex are two motives that have occurred to me. Hopefully, we'll discover the real reason tomorrow."

Toby was about to ask another question when he noticed the coroner's horse-drawn wagon arrive, followed closely by Bill Boyd's bright red Havers speedster.

"Please remain in your car, Mr. Boyd," Gressley said sternly.

"But my boss said to get a story about the body you found."

"You can have a story but not until the coroner has a chance to look at the body. Also, we don't want you walking around in the middle of a crime scene."

With no options, Bill remained in his car. About twenty minutes later, the body was wheeled to the wagon. Gressley walked over to Boyd's car. He explained that the victim was murdered and that his identity was unknown.

Bill asked, "When was he murdered?"

"Sometime between ten o'clock Saturday night and two o'clock this morning. Mr. Boyd, I wonder if you would do me a favor."

"What?"

Gressley asked, "Would the *Star* be able to circulate tomorrow's paper earlier than usual and run a description of the victim? We need to find out who he is as soon as possible."

"I'm sure we can do that."

After writing down all of the information, Bill asked Gressley if he would stand near the coroner's wagon for a photo.

Gressley replied, "Absolutely not."

"I'm cooperating with you; can't you do this little favor in return?"

Gressley smiled. "How about a compromise?" He motioned to Toby. "Tobias, please come here for a minute."

CHAPTER 7

▼

Bill Boyd ran a hand through his blond hair and sighed with satisfaction. He had just submitted two stories: the interview with Edgar Reynolds of the Michigan State Highway Department and the "Lighthouse Murder." Both of them would be on the front page of tomorrow's newspaper.

He looked at the clock. *It's seven o'clock,* he thought. *No wonder I'm hungry.* He walked over to the phone and dialed a familiar number.

"Hotel Marion, dining room."

"Hi, Clara. How's my favorite lady?"

"Fiddle, Mr. Boyd. You're making me blush."

Bill laughed. Clara was a tough, experienced waitress who hadn't blushed for twenty years. "I'm starved. Could you fix me a ham and cheese sandwich, a slice of apple pie, and a Coca-Cola? I would like to pick it up in about fifteen minutes."

"I think we can manage that. Working later than usual, are we?"

"Yes. I had a couple of important stories to complete for tomorrow's paper."

"I'll look forward to reading them. Your food will be waiting for you at the side door, as usual."

"Thanks."

Bill hung up the receiver, reattached the collar to his new Arrow shirt, and slipped on his jacket. As he was getting ready to leave his office, he remembered the conversation he had with Mary Sharpe earlier in the day. He returned to the phone and placed a long distance call to Ben Winchester, a reporter for the *Sarnia Observer,* a newspaper in Ontario, Canada.

After exchanging pleasantries, Bill said, "I had a conversation earlier today about young women being kidnapped in Canada and smuggled into the United States. As a Canadian, what's your opinion?"

"It's hard to tell," Ben said. "The police officers I've talked to think the numbers cited in the newspapers are way too high. When they track down a missing person's whereabouts, the police generally find that many had moved to another province or returned to their home in Europe."

"What about the ones who aren't found?"

Ben said, "There is one set of cases that might fit a kidnapping pattern. Many of the women not found within a month of their disappearance had migrated to Canada as individuals. Without other family members, nobody is as likely to report them missing right away. So they could be kidnapped and moved across the border before the police have a chance to find them."

"How many women fit that pattern?"

"The police estimate that there are about one hundred a year from the entire Ontario province. Of course, it might be that some of those women don't want to be found."

Bill asked, "Why not?"

"They might be in trouble with the police, or maybe they're hiding from an angry ex-boyfriend."

"Good point. Will you let me know if you have any more ideas on this?"

Ben said, "Will do. It sounds like an interesting idea for a story."

"I don't know where this is headed, but it is intriguing. Thanks for the information, and I hope your dinner didn't get cold."

Bill walked to the Marion Hotel, picked up his food, and slid into his car. As he was pulling out of the driveway, he thought, *I just might drive by the tunnel before I make up my mind about Mary's request.*

Minutes later, he stopped his car near the St. Clair River Railroad Tunnel. As he ate his sandwich, he thought about an article he had written to celebrate the tunnel's twentieth anniversary. Completed in 1891, it was probably one of the most remarkable engineering accomplishments in the Port Huron area. The tunnel was actually an iron tube twenty feet in diameter, more than a mile long, running underneath the St. Clair River. The tunnel contained the world's first international submarine railway, connecting the United States and Canada.

Special locomotives were built to pull the train cars through the tunnel. Because of the pollution problems associated with the old steam engines, locomotives were converted to electricity in 1908. Many celebrities, including Thomas Edison and Henry Ford, were in town to celebrate that event.

As Bill watched the tracks leading into the tunnel, he thought about the possibility of one hundred women being kidnapped in Canada and smuggled into the United States. He also thought about what a dramatic story he would have if he actually uncovered a kidnapping ring.

He slammed his hand on the car's steering wheel. He thought, *By Jove, I'll do it.*

*   *   *   *

Mary placed her book on the end table when she heard Toby walking toward the house. Toby dropped a large, shoebox-sized container with a shoulder strap on the floor and slumped into a chair. "You can't believe what just happened."

"What?"

Toby recounted the events at the Fort Gratiot Lighthouse. "And then Gressley made me pose for a picture. It will be in tomorrow's paper."

"That doesn't sound so bad."

"Then we went to the police station, and he explained that the chief put him in charge of the murder investigation, and that he could choose a patrolman to assist him. Can you believe it? He picked me. And after all the time I spend trying to avoid him."

Mary asked, "Aren't there people with more seniority?"

"That's what I said."

"And his answer?"

Putting on a grim expression, Toby tried to imitate Gressley's flinty voice. "Murders happen so rarely in Port Huron that no one has adequate training. I chose you because you appear to be quite trainable."

"Trainable!"

"That's what he said. Like I was a damn dog or something."

Mary laughed. "I'm sure he meant it as a compliment."

"You're probably right. He also said that the chief agreed that I was a good choice."

"Oh Toby, it will be a wonderful experience for you. What's in the box?"

Toby picked the box up and opened it. "This, my dear, is my detective kit, compliments of Detective Gressley. It's complete with a camera, a magnifying glass, and fingerprint material."

"Fingerprints?"

"Yes. Did you ever hear of the Thomas Jennings trial in Chicago a couple of years ago?"

"No."

Toby said, "Well, it was the first murder trial in the United States that finger-prints were permitted as evidence. Clarence Hiller had painted the railings to his house in the afternoon. Later in the day, someone shot him. When Thomas Jennings was arrested, his fingerprints matched the ones found on the wet paint. That evidence was used to help convict Jenkins."

"How exciting."

"The Illinois Supreme Court ruled that fingerprint evidence was admissible. When Gressley heard that, he spent a week in Chicago talking to the technicians at their Identification Bureau. He's really excited about using fingerprints in this case."

"How does it work?"

"Hand me the book you're reading."

Toby sprinkled a gray powder on the book. "This powder is mercury and chalk. Now I'll wipe it off lightly with this fancy brush."

"Good heavens! Those little curves are mine?"

"Yes. You have been found guilty of cramming your brain with Edith Whartonisms."

Mary laughed. "Oh my, officer! What's the punishment?"

"I'll let you off with a warning this time."

Mary reached in the box and took out the camera. "How do you get the crim-inal to pose?"

Toby said, "Very funny. Gressley wants me to take pictures of any crime scene. He's made arrangements with Clarence Smith from Smith's Photography to have photos developed within six hours."

"What kind of camera is it?"

Toby showed Mary how the maroon bellows opened up. He said, "That is a number three folding Brownie. It costs about fifty dollars."

"Goodness, that sounds expensive. Will it take pictures of fingerprints?"

"No. We need a more powerful camera for that, but no company is selling a commercial fingerprint camera."

Mary asked, "Then what can you do?"

"Gressley explained that all of the components to photograph fingerprints exist, but it would take a professional photographer to do it right. It turns out that Clarence volunteered to go to a crime scene and take pictures if we think it's necessary."

Noticing that Toby had begun strumming his fingers on the chair, Mary asked what was wrong.

"I know this is a great opportunity. But I just wish I felt more confident. I was also thinking about how some of the other patrolmen might react. I bet Wilbur Green's going to be upset. The way he brags, you would think he's the best cop in the department."

Mary reached over and held his hand. "Don't worry about Wilbur Green. Why don't we go upstairs and see if we can do something to help you unwind?"

Toby smiled as they walked to the stairs. He thought he felt more relaxed already.

CHAPTER 8

▼

Zizi heard a rooster crowing near the house. The shrill sound of the rooster reminded her of home, where a variety of farm animals wandered freely around the village. Her father, a government official in their village, had encouraged her to leave Hungary. He was convinced a war with Bosnia would start soon and that young women would be safer somewhere else. She wondered ruefully what he would think now.

She looked over at Soma, who had spent much of the night crying. Soma's beautiful eyes were puffy, and her face was streaked with tears and dirt. She looked like a helpless kitten, completely bewildered by her circumstances. Soma's frightened expression made Zizi resolve to so something.

Zizi looked around the dismal room for a sharp object with which she might be able to cut the ropes that were digging into her wrists and ankles. Using the wall as leverage, she managed to stand up. She hopped over to a desk in the corner. Standing with her back to the desk, she opened the drawers and felt for something sharp. In the third drawer, Zizi found a knife.

Zizi placed the knife between her hands and began to saw the ropes that bound her wrists. The awkward positioning soon caused pains in her wrists and fingers. But the knife was sharp enough that she could feel the strands on the rope begin to weaken. It took her about five minutes to cut through the rope. She ripped the gag off her mouth and whispered to Soma. "Have courage. We will soon be free."

Soma began to acknowledge Zizi, when her eyes suddenly expressed terror. Carl had entered the room. He said, "What do we have here, my little dears?"

Acting braver than she felt, Zizi pointed the knife at Carl. "Do not come near me, or I will use this."

Carl looked at Zizi's ankles, which were still tied. He burst out laughing. "You're going to hop over here and give me a poke with that knife, are you?" He walked over to Soma, and jerked her to her feet. He turned to Zizi. "I don't think you're going to do anything."

Zizi pleaded, "Please, do not hurt her."

Carl ripped Soma's blouse.

Zizi started toward Soma, lost her balance, and fell heavily to the floor. Still holding the knife, she tried frantically to cut the ropes on her ankles.

Carl gave Soma a lecherous look and groped her breasts. He said, "You better toss that knife away, or I don't know what might happen to your pretty little friend."

Zizi looked at Soma's wretched expression. She slid the knife across the floor and slumped against the wall in despair.

Charlie entered the room. "What's going on in here?"

Carl withdrew his hands from Soma. He said, "It seems like that little spitball over there was trying to get away. I got here just in time."

Charlie looked at Soma's torn blouse. He gave Carl a disgusted look. "Are you crazy? You know what the deal is. We can't deliver damaged goods. Now get out of here."

Carl sneered. "What does it matter? She's just going to marry some clodhopper in Kansas anyway." He stomped across the room and slammed the door shut as he left.

Charlie walked over to Zizi and retied her wrists. "Don't try anything like that again."

Zizi asked, "What is this clodhopper in Kansas?"

"I'll explain that later."

Zizi asked, "How long will we be here?"

"Just a few more hours. We'll be leaving here tonight."

"We cannot leave. Soma wants to marry Nikki."

"Nikki?"

"Yes. She was going to the dance hall to meet him when you captured us."

Charlie looked at Soma. "I'm sorry, but your future's going to be a little different than you planned."

After he tied and gagged Zizi, Charlie walked into the kitchen where Carl sat drinking a cup of coffee. "Carl, there are three things you need to do. First, go to a department store and buy new blouses, skirts, and undergarments for the girls. I want them to look nice when we deliver them. Second, don't molest them again. We don't have time for that kind of foolishness."

Carl said, "OK. What's the third thing?"

"Tell Nikki we won't need him tonight."

*　　　*　　　*　　　*

Toby kissed his family good-bye and walked toward the trolley line. He could not wait to get to the police station and begin working on the murder case. For the moment, however, he was preoccupied with a new adornment to his uniform. This was his first day wearing a zipper in the fly. Toby looked on the zipper as a fad that would never replace the reliable button fly. He could not believe that the department now required zippers for all uniforms.

Toby raised his leg cautiously as he boarded the trolley. He found a seat and settled in for the fifteen-minute ride to the police station. He had always worn his uniform with pride, but the zipper made him uncomfortable. Mary told him not to be silly, that nobody would notice. His children laughed at him when he squatted a few times and walked around the house like a gorilla with poison ivy on the inner parts of his legs.

Mary promised him that the zipper was sewn securely and would not come loose. But he was not so sure. He imagined how embarrassing it would be to look down during the middle of an interview and see his fly open.

Soon, however, his thoughts turned to the murder investigation. Who was the fat man that was killed? Why was he murdered? As his mind focused on these questions, Toby's concern about his zippered fly faded away.

*　　　*　　　*　　　*

Sylvia Pointe had already posted Toby's newspaper picture on the police department's bulletin board by the time he entered the station. She looked up from her desk. "Look who just walked in the door. The most adorable policeman in today's paper."

Sylvia was in her mid-thirties and a widow. She had worked as a secretary for the Port Huron police department for nearly fifteen years. One of the few female employees, she was more than able to hold her own with the frequent bantering that occurred in the office. Toby remembered their first encounter. She had greeted him with a loud voice and mischievous grin, and said, "So you're the new addition to the department. Can you type?" Despite the give-and-take of good-natured ribbing, Sylvia proved to be an invaluable asset when she assisted in some of the investigations. She needed to work to support herself, but Toby still thought married women should stay home to take care of their families.

Sylvia motioned toward Detective Gressley's door. She said, "Your master awaits."

Toby remembered what he had said last night about feeling like Gressley's pet dog and wondered if Sylvia had been eavesdropping at his house.

Toby poked his head into Gressley's office.

Gressley said, "Greeting Tobias. Are you ready to get to work? We already have some information."

"Yes, sir."

As Toby took a seat, Gressley offered him a cigarette. Toby declined.

"Never took up the nasty habit?" Gressley asked.

"No, sir."

Gressley said, "Tobias, would you do me a favor?"

"Yes, sir."

"Stop calling me sir."

Toby nodded, wishing he had the nerve to ask Gressley to stop calling him Tobias.

Gressley said, "Good. The evening desk clerk, a Mr. Phelps, from the Prince Albert Hotel called after seeing the article in this morning's paper. He said that a man fitting the description—five foot six and about 250 pounds—checked into the hotel Sunday. His name is Dexter Conroy, a businessman from Detroit. When the clerk read the article, he went to Mr. Conroy's room. It did not appear to have been slept in last night, and no one remembered seeing him Sunday. Mr. Phelps agreed to stay at the hotel until we could interview him more completely and have a look at Mr. Conroy's room."

"Why was Mr. Conroy in Port Huron?"

"Phelps thought he was here on business but did not know exactly what the business was."

"Any idea how he got to Port Huron?"

Gressley inhaled deeply on his cigarette. He said, "He arrived on the *Tashmoo*. Sylvia is calling Captain Baker to see if he can help us."

At the mention of her name, Sylvia rushed into Gressley's office. She said, "I just got off the phone with Captain Baker. He said he didn't have any information, but if someone wanted to board the *Tashmoo* at Marine City's Cherry Beach today, he would have the crew available for interviews."

Gressley pulled out his pocket watch and checked the time. He asked when the ship would be at Cherry Beach, and Sylvia told him the captain said he would make a special stop around eleven o'clock.

Gressley said, "Looks like if I hurry, I would be able to catch the 9:00 interurban. That would get me to Marine City in plenty of time."

Toby hesitated, and then asked, "What do you want me to do?"

Gressley said, "I want you to interview the desk clerk at the Prince Albert. Make sure you check for fingerprints in Conroy's room, especially around the door and window. Then go to the lighthouse and interview Frank Kimball. He was on duty the time of the murder and might have seen or heard something."

Toby asked, "You didn't interview him yesterday?"

"No. He was visiting relatives out of town."

Gressley turned to Sylvia. "I want you to call Conroy's business in Detroit and see if you can find out anything about him."

Gressley clapped his hands. "It looks like we all have plenty to do. I should be back in Port Huron by two o'clock. Let's meet back here at that time."

CHAPTER 9

▼

Bill Boyd led four of the newspaper's employees into the *Port Huron Star's* conference room and told them to help themselves to coffee and doughnuts and find a chair.

Henry Michaels grabbed a coffee and two doughnuts. "Must be something important—gettin' us to come in here and givin' us treats."

Bill flashed a quick grin. "Not much gets by you, does it Henry? And you're right, this is important. Did any of you read the recent AP article we printed on white slavery?"

Henry took a sip of coffee. "We get paid to work for the paper, not read it."

Richard Scott said, "Henry might be ignorant of what's going on in the world, but I read it."

Bill said, "Good. So at least some of you are aware that women are being smuggled into the United States from Canada."

Henry asked, "What kind of women?"

"According to an immigration inspector, they are mostly young, innocent women who are forced into prostitution or arranged marriages."

Henry leaned forward. "You mean a sixteen-year-old, like my little Nell, could be made to do those things?"

"I'm afraid so."

Richard asked, "Do you have any idea who's doing this?"

"I have no idea at all. But somebody locally might be involved."

Henry asked, "If that's happening, why ain't the government doing anything about it?"

Bill said, "Because it's too easy to get across the border. Some could come through the St. Clair Tunnel, but I imagine most are brought into the country on boats."

Henry said, "What are we goin' to do? Patrol the water all the way from Windsor to Sarnia?"

"No. I would like us to concentrate on the tunnel. It's one area we would be able to monitor rather easily."

Richard asked, "What do you want us to do?"

"I want you to take six-hour shifts watching the tunnel, starting noon today. I talked to the boss, and he agreed to give this a try for a month. We will cut your work time at the newspaper in half and double your wages. If nothing happens in a month, the project will be over. But if we get lucky, you'll all get a $100 bonus."

Henry slapped his hands on the table. "Let's get started! I'll take the first shift." The other men quickly volunteered for the other shifts.

Bill smiled broadly. "I knew I could count on you. It's important that you follow some simple rules. First, don't tell anybody what you're doing, not even members of your family. Tell them you're just working extra at the paper. Second, I'll furnish each of you with a train schedule. Make sure you are in a position to see the trains when they arrive. But don't stand in the same place all the time or you might arouse suspicion. Third, if you see anything out of the ordinary, call me. And above all, don't take unnecessary risks. If women are being smuggled into Port Huron, the people behind it are serious and dangerous."

*   *   *   *

The four-block walk from the police station to the Prince Albert Hotel necessitated crossing a bridge that spanned the Black River. Starting at the northwest corner of Port Huron, the Black River flows in a southern direction, creating the northwest boundary of the city. After a few miles, the river makes a forty-five degree turn, slicing through the center of Port Huron before it empties into the St. Clair River.

Not only does the Black River create a physical separation between the northern and southern sections of town, it also contributes to the confusion with street names. Toby was currently walking on Huron Avenue as he approached the Black River. Once across the drawbridge, he would be walking on Military Street. A couple blocks west, another bridge separated Seventh Street and Erie Street.

Toby's father speculated that the city officials in charge of street names were either drunk or had a weird sense of humor.

The Military Street drawbridge had recently been reinforced to withstand the weight of the city's trolley cars. Toby paused a minute on the bridge and watched a family of ducks wend their way around a variety of boats. He adjusted his detective kit and resumed his walk.

He entered the lobby of the Prince Albert Hotel and walked over to the desk. He knew that most of the younger people did not like the hotel's Victorian decor, considering it ostentatious and old-fashioned. But Toby liked the elaborate moldings and the dark, highly varnished woodwork. It reminded him of the house in which he was raised. Not as large at the Harrington or the Marion, the Prince Albert Hotel was an ideal location for someone who wanted privacy. Toby wondered if that might have been the main reason Mr. Conroy chose to stay there.

Toby approached the man at the desk and asked for Mr. Phelps. Mr. Phelps nodded and shook Toby's hand.

Toby said, "I'm Patrolman Tobias Sharpe. I'm here to see if you remember anything else about Mr. Conroy and to take a look at his room."

"Would you like some coffee?"

"Maybe just a little. I want to look at the room as soon as Clarence Smith gets here."

"The photographer?"

"Yes. He's going to help with the crime scene by photographing fingerprints."

As Phelps poured coffee, he said, "I'm afraid I don't know much about Mr. Conroy. As far as I know, this was the first time he stayed at our hotel."

Toby asked if he received any messages.

"I remember that someone left him a note Saturday night, sometime between seven and nine o'clock."

"You don't know exactly?"

Phelps said, "No. Someone placed it on the desk with Mr. Conroy's name on it. But I didn't see who put it there, so I'm not sure of the time. I just know it wasn't there when he came down to dinner at seven, and he picked it up when he went up to his room at nine."

"Was that the last time you saw him?"

"No. He left the hotel about eleven o'clock. He seemed really upset about something."

As Toby and Phelps were finishing their coffee, they watched an attractive young woman walk through the lobby and out the front door. Toby said, "Looks like your clientele is getting prettier."

"Her name's Charla. Let's just say she's someone else's client, if you know what I mean."

Toby said, "I don't know if you should be telling me something like that. I'm just here to investigate a murder." Toby turned as he saw Clarence.

Phelps introduced himself to Clarence and said he would show them to room 207.

They walked upstairs, and when he opened the room door, Mr. Phelps raised his voice. "What the hell happened in here?"

The room was in total disarray. Dresser drawers were pulled out and the contents scattered on the floor. The bed was torn apart. Toby noticed that the window had been broken from the outside. He leaned out the window. "Someone could have stood on that barrel, then grabbed the windowsill and pulled himself through the window."

Toby said, "Clarence, I want you to take pictures of the windowsill and the doorknob."

As Clarence assembled his camera, Toby dusted for fingerprints before he investigated the rest of the room. When Clarence was done photographing, Toby asked when the pictures would be developed.

Clarence said, "I'll have them at the police station by four o'clock."

Turning to Mr. Phelps, Toby asked if he could make a phone call.

Returning to the lobby, Toby called the police station. He heard a familiar voice.

"Sylvia, this is Toby. Someone broke into Mr. Conroy's room. Could you send someone over to maintain security until Detective Gressley can be consulted?"

Sylvia said, "I'll send somebody over right away. Toby, I got some important news."

"What?"

"We got a call from someone in the Lakeside Park area. He said his rowboat has been missing since Sunday morning. I don't know if it has anything to do with the murder, but you might want to check it out when you go to the lighthouse. I told them you would be there as soon as possible."

Toby wrote down the address and hurried out of the hotel to catch the city trolley. Since the police department did not own any motor cars, the easiest way to reach Lakeside Park was the electric trolley. The other options were walking, bicycling, or riding a horse. He hopped on the trolley and found a seat near the front.

Toby began thinking about his brief conversation with Sylvia. Her tone was always so confident, and she did her work efficiently. He thought it sometimes seemed like she was a member of the force instead of just a secretary. He also remembered how Gressley seemed to treat her as part of the investigation team this morning. *Maybe that's what happens when you work someplace for almost fifteen years,* he thought.

*   *   *   *   *

Luke Laboy waited for Charla in an alley, a block from the Prince Albert Hotel. He had watched Toby enter the hotel. He assumed that the police officer had been sent to investigate the break-in. He felt proud that he was responsible for making the police work. Now, as he watched Charla walk toward him, other feelings began to emerge in his fifteen-year-old body. It occurred to him that watching Charla was more exciting than looking at the lingerie section in the Sears and Roebuck catalog.

When she got near, Luke asked, "Did you get what you wanted?"

Charla looked upset. "No. I need your help again tonight. Could we meet at the Hotel Marion at about seven?"

"Sure."

Charla leaned closer and grasped Luke's arm. She whispered, "Remember, it's important that you don't tell anyone what we're doing, not even your brother."

Luke nodded his head vigorously. "Don't worry, I won't."

As Charla released his arm and turned to leave, her breasts brushed lightly against Luke's body.

Luke watched her walk down the street. He took a deep breath and began running, almost skipping, in the opposite direction.

*   *   *   *

Detective John Gressley had to sprint the last block to catch the nine o'clock interurban.

He sat down, waited for his breathing to return to normal, and lit a cigarette. He wondered for a moment what his Swiss Mennonite ancestors would think of his occupation and consumption of cigarettes. But, he enjoyed both of them too much to change, no matter what they might think.

For the first part of his trip, Gressley concentrated on the murder. He knew that he needed to consider evidence before spending a lot of time on motive. But so far, they had very little evidence. He wasn't even sure of the victim's identity.

Gressley's thoughts turned to Tobias Sharpe. It was Sylvia Pointe's idea that he ask the chief to assign Tobias as his assistant. Gressley knew the young man was smart, honest, and dedicated. But he was also inexperienced. Sylvia thought Tobias would do just fine, and he trusted her judgment. He wished that he had gone with Tobias to the Prince Albert Hotel, but the *Tashmoo* interview had to be done as soon as possible. He hoped that Tobias would not overlook anything.

As he watched the scenery along the interurban's route, he reflected on the convenience of this form of travel. This particular route ran between Port Huron and Detroit and took about four hours to complete. It began operation about twelve years ago, a few years before Gressley moved to Port Huron.

When he looked at a map of the interurban in southeastern Michigan, it reminded him of a giant octopus, with the body being located in Detroit and Windsor, Canada. The lines to the Michigan cities of Port Huron, Imlay City, Flint, Pontiac, and Ann Arbor as well as Toledo, Ohio, and the Canadian cities of Amherstberg and Leamington represented the tentacles.

He liked going to Detroit, with its various forms of entertainment. It also allowed him to romance Sylvia without too many people knowing. They would enjoy dinner, a show, and then stay overnight. They agreed that when in Port Huron, they would try to keep their relationship as private as possible.

Sylvia was eager to see Mae West, a rising star of vaudeville. Her sensual dancing and singing were outrageous, and her dialogue was a humorous lampooning of Victorian values. Mae West was coming to Detroit next month, and Sylvia wanted Gressley to get tickets.

Gressley reflected on the difference between Sylvia and his first wife, Bernice. He and Bernice were both in their early twenties when they married. Bernice assumed that their marriage would be a duplicate of her parents, one based on nineteenth-century Victorian customs. When it became apparent that Gressley was not a stand-in for her father, the relationship became strained. But divorce was out of the question. State laws would not allow a divorce simply because of incompatibility.

That is, divorce was out of the question until a woman Gressley arrested accused him of sexually molesting her. The charge was absurd, but Bernice seized on the accusation as an excuse to file for a divorce on the grounds of adultery. Gressley found himself in a terrible dilemma. If he fought the charge, he would remain in a marriage neither he nor his wife wanted. If he did not contest the charge of adultery, his career would be severely damaged. Gressley decided it was better to damage his career than remain in a loveless marriage.

Fortunately, his friends were able to help him get a job in Port Huron. When he accepted the job, he had to start at a lower rank, earn less money, and have fewer challenging crimes to investigate. He had hoped to find a position as a detective, but the Port Huron police department had no such category. The best it could do was offer a job as a sergeant. Five years later, the department created the special rank of detective for him. He knew that if he were in a larger city, he would have already earned the rank of lieutenant. But, after spending eight years in Port Huron, he had achieved a level of contentment.

As the interurban neared Marine City, Gressley introduced himself to a couple seated next to him. "Good morning, I'm John Gressley."

The man shook Gressley's hand. "Good morning. I'm George, and this is my wife, Marie."

"Are you familiar with Marine City?"

"Yes. We live near there."

Gressley asked, "Would you be able tell me how to get to Cherry Beach?"

"Sure. It's about a mile south of where we're going to get off."

Gressley wrote the directions in his notebook and thanked him.

George said, "You're welcome." He paused for a moment before continuing. "Excuse me for being bold but were you at the Majestic Theater Saturday night?"

"Yes."

"I thought so. We sat right behind you and your wife."

Gressley coughed. He said, "It was an enjoyable show, but I was just thinking about the big-name performers that appear in Detroit."

"Oh yes," Marie said. "I especially like Will Rogers."

George said, "I hear Harry Houdini has a new escape routine called the Chinese Water Torture Cell."

"I read about that," Gressley replied. "It sounds like a dangerous act."

Marie said, "I think some acts are getting too risqué. From what I understand, that young entertainer Mae West does a seductive cooch dance that is just sinful." She leaned closer to Gressley, and whispered, "I think she should have stayed in burlesque."

Gressley gave a noncommittal nod and stood up as the interurban came to a stop.

He walked into a general store to buy some cigarettes. He asked for a pack of Lucky Strikes.

"Sorry fella," the clerk said. "We're all out, and the delivery wagon won't be here until noon. Would you like to try some Fatimas? They're not very popular, but I think you'll like them."

"Sure, I'll give them a try." He slid the cigarette tin into his suit jacket and left the store to continue his walk to Cherry Beach.

CHAPTER 10

▼

Mary Sharpe sat in her kitchen, peeling potatoes. When the phone rang, she plunged the paring knife into an unsuspecting potato, wiped her hands on her apron, and answered the phone.

"Hi Mary, this is Bill Boyd. I decided to honor your request regarding the slave trade surveillance."

"Oh, that's wonderful."

"I hired four men to stand six-hour shifts. That way, the railroad tracks will be monitored twenty-four hours a day."

"Is the newspaper sponsoring this?"

"No. I decided to pay for it myself. What's the point of having money if you can't throw some of it around?"

"You're a rascal but a good one. When do they start?"

Bill said, "The first shift starts at noon today. I'm going to try it for a month to see what happens."

"Did you tell them not to talk to anyone about what they're doing?"

"Indeed I did. I made it very clear that if other people know what they were doing, it would ruin the whole project."

Mary said, "Let's hope it works."

"If it does, I'll have a great story for the paper. Are you going to contact any federal agencies?"

"We have meetings scheduled with the Life-Saving Service tomorrow and the Customs Service Wednesday."

Bill said, "Good luck. Oh, by the way, how did you like Toby's picture in the newspaper this morning?"

"I thought it was wonderful. Toby was a little self-conscious about it though. He's afraid he's getting in over head because of his lack of experience."

"He'll do all right. Detective Gressley wouldn't have picked him if he didn't think Toby could handle it."

"That's what I told him last night."

"I just talked to Sylvia Pointe to see if there was any new information about the murder. We joked around for a while, but she wouldn't tell me anything."

Mary laughed. "Do you think she would give any information to a nosy reporter?"

Bill released a loud, prolonged sigh. "Mary, you have cut me to the quick. Do you mean to say that you don't trust the newspapers?"

Mary smiled, knowing that he was teasing. "Good heavens Bill, have I hurt your feelings? Would an invitation to dinner at six o'clock make up for it? I'm making potato salad."

"You're forgiven. I'll be there. I haven't had a square meal for days."

*   *   *   *

Sylvia took the Detroit phonebook to her desk. Within minutes she found the only business listed for Conroy. She rang the switchboard and placed a long distance call to Detroit. As she waited, she thought about Bill Boyd's visit earlier in the morning. *I really enjoy Bill's company*, she thought. But did he really think I would tell him anything about the investigation? It was a good thing Toby and John had already left, or he might have tried to follow them. Her thoughts were interrupted by a voice on the other end of the line.

"Conroy Enterprises, Maude speaking."

"Good morning Maude, this is Sylvia Pointe from the Port Huron police department."

"How can I help you?"

"We're investigating the murder of a man who might possibly be your employer."

"Dexter Conroy?"

Sylvia said, "Yes. We found the body of a man in his fifties. About five foot six and 250 pounds."

"Good heavens. Does the body have a moustache?"

"Yes, and he apparently didn't sleep at the Prince Albert Hotel last night. Do you know if Mr. Conroy was planning to come to Port Huron?"

Maude said, "Yes. I made arrangements on the *Tashmoo* for him. He was supposed to come back tomorrow. I'm shocked. He wasn't my favorite person, but I am sorry to hear that he might be dead. Are you sure it's him?"

"Not entirely. So far no one has identified the body. Can you tell me anything about Mr. Conroy? I just have a couple of quick questions."

"Are you a policewoman?"

Sylvia said, "No, but I've been told to call your office to get as much information as possible."

"Gee, I really would like to help, but this is my day off. I just came in to take care of a few things. I'm already late for a suffragette séance."

Sylvia asked, "A what?"

"A group of us are getting together to see if we can resurrect the issue from the dead. I spent over ten years on that project, and I'm not about to give up yet."

"Me either. I think it's a damn shame that the only people who could vote on whether women could have the right to vote were men! Do you think this state-by-state strategy to get the vote is going to work?"

Maude said, "It sure didn't work in Michigan. But at least Illinois and several western states decided the right way. I just hope I live long enough to be treated as a rational adult who's competent enough to vote."

"We can't give up now. Anyway, I've kept you long enough. The department will be calling you back if we are able to determine that the dead man is actually your employer."

"Look, I'm already late, and they can't start levitating without me. What do you need to know?"

Sylvia said, "What do you know about his business?"

"He invests in different things. He's pretty open about some of it, but he keeps a lot of what he does secret from me."

"Is he working on any current deal?"

"Yes," Maude said. "But he hasn't said anything about it. The only thing I know is that he's received several phone calls from Lansing recently."

"Do you know who he talked to?"

"No. The caller would never give his name."

Sylvia asked, "I know this is a delicate area, but between two suffragettes, is there anything you can tell me about Mr. Conroy's private life?"

"Not much."

Disappointment was apparent in Sylvia's voice. "Oh."

"Not much that's good anyway. The bad will take about two hours."

Sylvia laughed. "Maybe you could give me the abridged version."

"For one, he's in the process of getting a divorce."

Sylvia paused, thinking momentarily about the unfortunate situation John Gressley had endured. She asked, "What would the grounds for a divorce be? Did she commit adultery?"

"Heaven's no. Mr. Conroy is accusing the poor woman of being a habitual drunk."

"Is she?"

Maude said, "She drinks a lot, and I suppose Mr. Conroy can pay people to testify that she's a drunk. Do you know she lives in Port Huron?"

"No. What's the address?"

"They have a cottage along Lake Huron. Mrs. Conroy stays up there from May through October. I think it's mostly to stay away from Mr. Conroy. I called her Friday to tell her that her husband was coming to Port Huron and wanted to discuss the divorce issue with her on Sunday. They were going to meet in his room at the Prince Albert Hotel."

"Why not meet at their home?" Sylvia asked.

"He hates going there. She's the one who insisted on the house on Lake Huron. He went along with it as long as she didn't try to interfere with his social life. He has close female friends."

"Is that the reason why he wants a divorce?"

"Yes," Maude said. "He was pretty serious about a young woman by the name of Charlotte Clemons—or maybe the last name was Clements. But something happened about two weeks ago that broke up that relationship. This Charlotte woman came to the office last week and they got into a heated argument. He called her a wicked name that I won't repeat and said he never wanted to see her again. She threw a vase at him and stormed out."

"What does she look like?"

"She's tall, mid-twenties, blue eyes, and dark hair. She's very pretty but sort of hard-looking for someone so young."

Sylvia asked, "Do the Conroys have any children?"

"They have a son, Dexter Jr. Mr. Conroy has been in a constant feud with his son over gambling debts. Seems that Dexter Jr. goes to some local club called the Tarantula. He thinks he's a good poker player. He's either pretty bad or has terrible luck. He owes thousands of dollars."

"Who does he owe the money to?"

"A professional gambler by the name of Slick Finley," Maude said. "Let me tell you, he's not the kind of person you want to owe money to. His dad paid some of his debts but refuses to pay any more of them."

"So Mr. Conroy and his son don't get along?"

"That's an understatement. Dexter Jr. thinks he's entitled to almost anything, while Mr. Conroy sees him as a spoiled, lazy brat."

Sylvia said, "It sounds like Mr. Conroy had a lot of enemies."

"He sure does. Is that all, Sylvia? I really do need to go to that meeting."

"Thanks for the information and give my regards to our kindred spirits."

CHAPTER 11

▼

Toby stood on the porch of the address he had been given. Before he could knock, a short, bald man opened the screen door and walked outside. Toby said, "I'm patrolman Toby Sharpe. Are you Mr. Brown?"

"That's me, and you must be the policeman whose picture was in the newspaper today."

Toby blushed.

"I'm sorry we called you because I found my boat just a few minutes ago. We found it at Lakeside Park."

"I'm happy that you got your boat back. When do you think it was stolen?"

Mr. Brown scratched his bald head. "I know it was here when we went to bed last night. That was about ten o'clock."

Toby asked, "Did you hear any noises after you went to bed?"

"No. Nothing special."

"Do you mind if I examine your boat?"

Mr. Brown said, "Nope. We left it at the park. I thought you might want to look at it for clues."

"I sure do. Where is it in the park?"

"It's right in front of the concession stand. You can't miss it. It's got my name painted on the bow."

Toby thanked the bald man and began to leave. As he was walking down the porch steps, Mr. Brown called him. Toby turned around to face Mr. Brown. Mr. Brown said, "I've been thinking about that murdered man described in today's paper. He sounds a lot like Dexter Conroy. He owns the house three doors north of here."

Toby's eyes widened. "That's interesting. Do you know anything about him?"

"Not much. He's not around here very often, but his wife stays here most of the summer. You might want to talk to Ed and Catherine. They live next door to the Conroy house. From what I understand, they've heard quite an earful."

Toby shook Mr. Brown's hand and thanked him.

Toby walked quickly to the white house with green shutters described by Mr. Brown and knocked on the door. When Catherine answered the door, Toby said, "I'm Patrolman Toby Sharpe, and I wondered if you would answer a few questions about your neighbors, the Conroys?"

Catherine opened the door. "Certainly. Please come in." Nodding to a man sitting on the sofa, Catherine said, "This is my husband, Ed. How can we help you?"

"We're investigating a murder and believe that the victim might have been your neighbor, Mr. Conroy."

Ed pointed to the newspaper on the footstool. "I was just reading the article in today's paper. And you must be the young man on the front page."

Toby felt like he was never going to have his picture taken again. He said, "That's me. Now what could you tell me about the Conroy family?"

Catherine said, "They've been our neighbors for about two years. Mr. Conroy isn't here very often; he spends most of his time in Detroit."

"That's right," Ed said. "And when he is here, he spends a lot of time arguing with his wife and son."

"What do they argue about?"

"The arguments with the son had mostly to do with money," Catherine said. "It sounded like Dexter Jr. had huge gambling debts. The last time Dexter Sr. was here, I heard him say that he was not going to give his son any more money."

"What did Mr. Conroy and his wife argue about?"

"Sometimes it would be about having to come to Port Huron," Ed said. "He hated it here. The last couple of times, it had to do with her drinking. But Catherine and I agreed that it seems like he was doing it for the neighbors' benefit."

"How do you mean?"

Catherine said, "Well, it seemed like he would wait until she was in her rose garden. Then he would come outside and talk in a very loud voice. It was like he wanted us to hear that he was upset about her drinking."

"What are Mrs. Conroy and the son like?"

"The son's not very nice," Ed said. "He resented living in Port Huron. He was always complaining about not having anything to do. But his father made it clear that he didn't want Dexter Jr. living in Detroit."

"What about the mother?"

"I felt sorry for her," Catherine said. "She was friendly enough when she first moved here, but her behavior has become increasingly erratic over the past year."

"How so?"

Ed said, "Moody. Some days she would be angry. Then other days she would be just fine."

Toby said, "Thanks for your help. I think I'll go next door and talk to the Conroys."

Catherine said, "I'm afraid you won't be able to do that. They left in Dexter Jr.'s car about a half hour ago."

Toby walked along the beach toward Lakeside Park. *Great,* he grumbled to himself. *I won't be able to impress Gressley with an interview of the Conroys. Maybe I'll have better luck with the boat.*

*   *   *   *

Albert and Mildred Fleming entered a Toronto police station and walked determinedly to the front desk. The constable on duty smiled cordially and said, "May I be of assistance?"

Albert said, "Two of our boarders have been missing since Saturday night, and we're afraid they're in trouble."

"Why do you think that?"

"Because they're good girls who have never done anything like this before," Mildred said. "And when we called the factory where they're employed, the foreman said they did not report to work this morning. They've never missed a day of work since they started last year."

The constable stood up. "Please wait here. I'll get Detective Alexander."

Within minutes the constable returned to the desk, accompanied by a short, stocky man with a receding hairline. The constable introduced them.

Detective Alexander shook their hands and invited them to his office. The Flemings followed Alexander into his office and sat in two wooden chairs.

Alexander sat behind his desk and picked up a pencil. He said, "I understand you have two young female boarders who did not return Saturday night and did not show up for work this morning. Is that correct?"

Mildred said, "Yes. They are employed at the Winslow Shirt Company."

"What are their names?"

Albert said, "Soma Fekete and Zizi Balogh. They immigrated to Canada from Hungary last year and have been staying with us since they arrived in Toronto."

"Describe them, please."

Mildred said, "They are in their early twenties. They both have dark hair and brown eyes. Soma is a little taller than average and is very attractive. Zizi is average height and cute."

"What were they wearing when you last saw them? Did they take any other clothes with them when they went to work Saturday?"

Mildred twisted her handkerchief nervously. "They wore black skirts and white blouses. They didn't take any other clothes with them when they went to work." Mildred paused for a moment and looked at her hands. "They're nice girls, detective."

Alexander smiled. "I'm sure they are Mrs. Fleming. But young women often have a social life. What do they do on weekends? Do they have boyfriends?"

"They often go dancing Saturday nights," said Mildred. "Zizi has been teasing Soma about somebody called Nikki. I think they met him at a dance hall."

"Do you know where they go dancing?"

Albert said, "They've been talking about the Imperial Ball Room the last couple of months."

Detective Alexander stood up. "You did the right thing reporting this. I'll check into it, and if we discover anything, I'll be in contact with the two of you."

Albert shook the detective's hand and thanked him.

*   *   *   *

Gressley reached Cherry Beach near Marine City about fifteen minutes before the *Tashmoo* was scheduled to arrive. He sat on a bench next to an elderly man. He nodded to a steamer heading north, its bow knifing through the blue waters of the St. Clair River. "I can't believe how big those ships have become in the last few years."

The elderly man pulled a plug of tobacco from his pocket and bit off a chaw. "That's the *Charles S. Price*."

"How can you tell from this distance?"

"Very few freighters are 524 feet long and fifty-four feet at the beam. It's huge."

"Over 500 feet," Gressley said. "That's almost two football fields, end to end."

The old man nodded. "Of the freighters that long, only a couple have such a large, white forecastle. It looks a lot like the *Isaac M. Scott*, but I know for a fact that the *Scott* went by just a couple of days ago."

"What do you think she's carrying?"

The old man spit into a tin can. "Probably a load of coal."

"You watch the ships often?"

The old man held up his gnarled fingers. "Quit farming when the 'ritis got too painful. My son brings me here about three times a week to watch the ships. Fifty years ago, I was on the battlefields with General Grant. Now it's hard just to milk a cow." He paused and then asked, "You from around these parts?"

"Port Huron. I'm here to catch the *Tashmoo.*"

"Looks like you're out of luck, sonny. It used to stop here but not this year."

Gressley said, "I know, but Captain Baker agreed to stop today because of special circumstances."

The old man looked at Gressley quizzically. "What are you, some kind of bigwig?"

"Hardly. But I'm doing some important police business. There was a murder Sunday night, and we think the victim came to Port Huron on the *Tashmoo.*"

The old man nodded. "I hope you find what you're looking for." He then pointed toward the water. "Here comes the *Tashmoo* now. Ain't she a beaut?"

Gressley agreed. Because of the *Tashmoo*'s sleek appearance, she was often referred to as "the prettiest girl on the Great Lakes." It had three decks that were gleaming white. The main distraction was the two smoke stacks spewing black smoke. With a capacity of 3,500 passengers, the 300-foot-long ship made daily trips between Detroit and Port Huron during the summer.

He boarded the ship and introduced himself to Captain Baker.

"Ah, welcome aboard Detective Gressley."

Captain Baker took Gressley toward the *Tashmoo*'s B-deck salon. "We had more than 2,500 people on the ship Saturday. The majority of passengers, about 1,500, got off at Tashmoo Park."

"How long of a ride is that?" Gressley asked.

"It's about thirty miles north of Detroit. With all the picnic areas and other amusements there, it makes a wonderful getaway for families. We pick them up on our return trip to Detroit."

"What about the other thousand?"

"About a third of those, mostly older people, stay on the ship the entire time. We leave Detroit at 9:00 AM and return about 8:00 PM. They're able to enjoy a fine lunch and dinner as they watch the beautiful scenery. We even have some lovely cabins for couples who want more privacy. The rest of the passengers got off at various stops."

The two men entered the salon. Gressley remarked on the attractive furnishings in the salon.

Captain Baker rubbed his hand along the back of a highly polished, ornate chair. "It looked a lot better thirteen years ago when everything was new. But, it still looks nice, doesn't it?"

Captain Baker and Gressley approached two young men who were introduced as Jimmy Erickson and Pete Richmond. "Jimmy is a waiter," Captain Baker said. "So, perhaps you could interview him first because lunch will be served in about an hour."

Gressley agreed, and the men went to a table in the corner.

Captain Baker said, "Would you like some coffee?"

Gressley said, "Thanks, that would hit the spot right now."

Gressley took a sip of coffee. It had a wonderful bitter taste. He removed the tin of Fatimas from his pocket. When he opened the tin, he noticed a baseball card. Gressley picked up the card and showed it to Jimmy. "Do you save these?"

"No. Boxing's the sport I like."

Gressley offered the tin to Jimmy. "Would you like a cigarette?"

"No sir. Captain Baker doesn't like the waiters smokin' while on duty. Makes for a bad image."

Gressley shrugged his shoulders, lit up, and inhaled deeply.

"Now, could you describe Mr. Conroy?"

"Well, he was really fat. He kind of reminded me of ex-President Taft—only shorter. He had that same kind of bushy moustache as Taft."

"Did you talk to him?"

Jimmy said, "Yes, sir. I was his waiter. He looked rich, so I thought if I was real friendly I might get a big tip. So I asked him what he was going to do in Port Huron. He said he planned on watching some horse races at Driving Park when we got there Saturday. That famous horse, Dan Patch, was on the racing card, and Mr. Conroy wanted to see if he's as good as they claim."

Gressley smiled. "I think he is. He won all three heats."

"After we talked about horse racing for a while, I made a mistake of asking him what he thought of the *Tashmoo*."

"Why was that a mistake?"

"Because he got real high falootin', saying how it didn't hold a candle to the great ocean liners. That got my dander up, so I said, 'At least it didn't sink on its maiden voyage, like that *Titanic* did last year.'"

"I bet he didn't like that." Gressley tapped his cigarette.

"No sir. He looked at me like I was some cockroach or something. Then he frowned and told me to just be quiet and bring his food."

"Did he give you much of a tip?"

Jimmy said, "No, but he didn't get the best service either."

"Well, Jimmy, I'm a generous tipper. Do you think you might find me a table in the dining room and provide your best service?"

"Yes, sir, the whitefish looks really good today. How about twelve-thirty?"

"That would be fine. Now, would you ask Pete to come over?"

Gressley watched a small, pencil-thin boy walk shyly toward him. His tiny stature made his large nose appear enormous.

"Morning, sir," he said. He sat on the edge of the chair, looking like a red-billed toucan ready to take flight.

"How old are you?"

"Fifteen. I know I'm small for my age. My dad says that someday my body will grow enough to catch up with my nose."

Gressley smiled. "Do you remember seeing Mr. Dexter Conroy?"

"Yes. I took care of his baggage when he boarded."

"Did he give any special instructions?"

Pete said, "Just that he wanted the suitcase delivered to the Prince Albert Hotel."

"Did you see him any other time?"

"Yes. He was smoking on C Deck just about this time Saturday."

Gressley asked, "Anything happen?"

"This other man came up and started talking. Pretty soon they were arguing. I was close enough to hear the fat man say they would talk later but didn't want to be seen together once they got to Port Huron. Then he noticed me and turned away."

"Do you remember what the other man looked like?"

Pete said, "He had red hair with lots of freckles. And he had a big Adam's apple that went up and down when he got excited. Let me tell you, it was really bobbin' during their argument."

"Anything else you can remember?"

"When I took Mr. Conroy's suitcase off the ship in Port Huron, one of the latches was open."

Gressley asked, "Is that unusual?"

"It doesn't happen very often."

"Would other passengers have had access to his suitcase?"

Pete said, "I suppose. There's no guard, and the area's not locked."

"Thanks."

Pete stood up and nodded shyly toward the baseball card on the table. "Detective Gressley, are you going to keep that card?"

"No. Would you like to have it?"

"Yes sir. That's part of the T200 series produced by the Ligget and Myers Tobacco Company. They made sixteen cards, one for each major league team. That's the St. Louis Browns, one of the hardest cards to find."

Gressley handed the card to Pete. "Glad to be of service."

Pete gushed, "Gee, thanks."

Gressley smoked another cigarette as he walked slowly around the ship. Arriving at the dining room at exactly twelve-thirty, he took his seat, and enjoyed a lunch of whitefish, potatoes au gratin, a delicate Chardonnay, and the most delicious chocolate cake he had ever tasted.

*   *   *   *

Toby walked up to the Lakeside Park concession stand and ordered two hot dogs and a bottle of Vernors ginger ale. He found a bench facing Lake Huron and sat down heavily. The investigation of Mr. Brown's rowboat was a big disappointment. The oar handles had been wiped clean. He used his magnifying glass to examine the entire boat but did not find anything that seemed helpful. He wondered if Sherlock Holmes actually found any clues with his magnifying glass.

Toby bit into his hot dog and looked at beautiful Lake Huron. He had never seen an ocean, but as he looked eastward across the lake, he imagined that it must be something like this. No land, only water, all the way to the horizon. He had always been intrigued with how colors on the lake surface would change from emerald green to various shades of blue to icy gray. On windy days, the water would have multiple colors. Near the shore, the wind would stir up the sand, causing the water to be brown. Farther from the shore, the water would be a deep blue.

Anchored about five miles off shore was the federal lightship, staffed by members of the United States Life-Saving Service. One of the main responsibilities of the Service in this area was to safely guide ships in and out of Lake Huron as it empties into the St. Clair River, where the strong currents are particularly treacherous. The lightship functioned as a floating lighthouse. Toby had always wondered what it would be like to be stationed on a ship that remained anchored in one place all the time.

When he was in high school, he thought about joining the Life-Saving Service. He remembered the brochure saying that in addition to helping ships, the Service was responsible for enforcing anti-smuggling laws. He thought it sounded like an exciting life. But he didn't like the idea that he might be stationed some-place other than Port Huron.

Toby fed the remaining portion of his hot dog bun to the squawking seagulls. Shifting his gaze to the south, he looked in the direction of the Fort Gratiot Lighthouse, which stood at the mouth of the St. Clair River. *Might as well walk,* he thought. *The exercise will do me some good.* He finished his ginger ale, threw the bottle into a refuse container, and began walking toward the lighthouse.

The lighthouse soon came into view. Nearly ninety feet tall, the cylin-der-shaped building was painted white with a red dome. When the lighthouse was originally built in 1829, it was nearly seventy feet tall. After sailors com-plained they could not see the light clearly, an extra twenty feet were added in the 1860s. Toby could see the seam where the upper part was attached. A house for the keeper of the lighthouse was built in the 1870s.

Toby knocked on the door. Frank Kimball, who had served as keeper of the lighthouse since 1900, poked his head out of one of the lighthouse's windows. He said, "I'm up here. I saw you walking along the beach and figured you would want to talk to me."

"That's right, Mr. Kimball. I'm Patrolman Toby Sharpe."

"Are you related to Otis and Ruth Sharpe?"

"Yes. I'm their son."

Mr. Kimball said, "Well, I'll be darned. It's good to see young people sticking around here instead of taking off for the big cities. You know, you look like your dad. What can I do for you?"

"I have a few questions about last night's murder."

"I don't know if I can help but come on up."

Toby entered the lighthouse, climbed the circular stairs, and found Kimball standing on the balcony that encircled the structure. He asked, "You climb these steps every day?"

"I go up and down those ninety-four steps at least four times a day. Have to make sure the light stays in good working order. Sometimes I have to come up in the dark, if the wind blows the light out." Toby stepped out onto the balcony and immediately grabbed the railing. He said, "I thought I was going to fall."

Mr. Kimball laughed. "A lot of people have that feeling. The platform is tilted so that when it rains, the water will drain away from the lighthouse."

Still holding on the railing, Toby said, "Detective Gressley wanted me to ask you about Saturday night. Do you remember seeing or hearing anything unusual?"

"I heard some noises about midnight. Sounded like a couple of people arguing. I got out of bed, turned on the light, and looked out the window, but I couldn't see anything."

Toby asked, "Could you tell anything about the voices? Did they sound old or young? Could you tell if they were male or female?"

"I couldn't tell. It was too far away."

"Do you remember anything else?"

Mr. Kimball said, "Well, I seem to remember a rowboat up on the shore. It was about a block from the lighthouse, close to those trees over there. It wasn't there when I got up Sunday morning."

Toby descended the stairs. "Thanks for your time."

"You're welcome. Say hi to your parents."

Toby boarded the trolley and headed back to the station.

CHAPTER 12

▼

Detective Alexander stood in front of a secretary's desk at the Winslow Shirt Company. The secretary peered over her glasses. "May I help you?"

"I'm Detective Cedric Alexander of the Toronto police. I have an appointment to see the foreman on the second floor."

The secretary pointed to the stairway. "Go up those stairs to the second floor and ring the bell. Mr. Lewis will see you there."

He thanked her. Once on the second floor, Alexander walked to the door leading to the work area. It was locked. He rang the bell and waited several minutes. Finally, Mr. Lewis opened the door and looked at him suspiciously. "What do you want?"

"I'm Detective Cedric Alexander, and I want to talk to you about two young women who work on your floor—Soma Fekete and Zizi Balogh."

"Oh, yeah. I was told you were coming."

Alexander entered the work area. He asked, "Why do you have the door locked?"

"You can't trust these women. Most of them are foreigners who would steal us blind if we're not careful. We don't let them out until the shift ends."

"But what happens if there's a fire? Didn't the tragedy at the Triangle Factory in New York teach you anything? One hundred and fifty workers burned to death in that fire."

Lewis grunted. "That won't happen here. First of all, we're only a four-story building. The women who got killed at the Triangle were on the eighth floor. Plus, we've got a better sprinkler system than theirs."

Alexander looked at the women's sad faces. "It must be degrading to be locked in when you come to work. Seems like some kind of prison."

"Are you here to talk about working conditions or to ask about Soma and Zizi?"

"Maybe we should talk about both. But let's focus on the missing girls for now. I understand they didn't show up for work today. Is that unusual for them?"

"Yeah. This is the first day they missed since they started working here. And they work harder than most of the girls. But you never know about these foreigners. They might have found another job, or maybe they're havin' a long weekend with some big spender."

Alexander asked, "Do you know what they do on weekends?"

"No, I don't know anything about their private lives. You could ask Emily. She works beside them."

"Which one is Emily?"

"She's the heavyset blond at the end of the second table. If you don't have any more questions for me, I need to get back to work." Without waiting for a reply, Lewis turned and walked away.

Alexander walked over to Emily and introduced himself. "I want to ask you a few questions about Soma Fekete and Zizi Balogh."

Emily stopped her machine. "I haven't seen them since Saturday when we left this sweatshop."

"Do you have any idea what they might have been planning to do?"

"I don't know for sure, but they've been talking about the Imperial Ball Room a lot lately."

Alexander asked, "Did either of them have a boyfriend?"

"Zizi's been teasing Soma about somebody named Nikki. That's all I know."

"Do you know what this Nikki looks like?"

Emily said, "Zizi said he was tall, parted his hair in the middle, and was good-looking. But I guess that sounds like a lot of people, doesn't it?"

Alexander smiled as he patted his receding hairline. "I'm afraid your description would eliminate some of us. Thank you for the information."

As Alexander turned to leave, Emily asked, "Do you think something bad happened to them? Were they murdered or kidnapped?"

"It's too early to jump to conclusions but those are possibilities."

Emily started her sewing machine. "I've been reading about that white slavery thing, and it would be terrible if that's what happened to them."

*   *   *   *

In 1913, Sperry's department store was located at the southeast corner of Huron Avenue and Butler Street. A large awning traversed the entire west side of the building. J. B. "Ben" Sperry opened a hardware store in 1893. By 1913, it had been transformed into a department store.

Charla entered Sperry's and walked directly to the hosiery display. She chose two pairs of plain cotton hose and looked for a clerk. As she turned around, she noticed a gorgeous pair of black silk stockings. Embroidered on each stocking was a snake. When worn, the head of the snake would be on the top of the foot, with its eyes facing the toes. The snake's body would wind around the leg, up to the knee. Charla added these to her purchase.

After leaving the store, Charla glanced across the street where she saw the advertisement for the Majestic Theater's production of *Henpecked Henry*. She smiled grimly as she thought that half of the married men she serviced were henpecked.

Charla stiffened as she saw Dexter Conroy Jr. leave the bank and head down Huron Avenue. She would never forgive Dexter for not fighting for her last year. Charla blamed his cowardliness for much of her current unhappiness. No matter how tough Dexter Jr. tried to act, she knew that he was weak.

But as she watched him enter Fisherman's Tavern, it occurred to her that she might be able to manipulate him. She took a deep breath and entered the smoke-filled, dingy tavern. Dexter was sitting in a booth near the door. Charla walked over and said hello.

Dexter's eyes widened. "Charla! What are you doing in Port Huron?"

"Just tying up some loose ends. Can I join you?"

Dexter jumped up, tipping over his chair as he seated her across from him. He said, "You sure can. My treat."

Charla hid her irritation. *Now you want to spend money on me?* she thought.

The waitress appeared and asked if they were ready to order.

Charla said, "A salad and hot tea, please."

Dexter ordered a roast beef sandwich, American-fried potatoes, and a bottle of Kern's Cream of America beer. He said, "One good thing about this rinky-dink town is that beer. Did you know it won the grand prize at the Paris Exhibition in 1911?"

"I've heard that."

Dexter said, "Did you hear about Dad?"

Charla played with her silverware for a moment. "Was that him described in this morning's paper?"

"Yeah. Mom and I identified the body just a couple of hours ago."

"Are you and your mom OK?"

"I guess so. We both had our problems with Dad. Now Mom's got her rose garden to take care of, and I'm free of his control."

Charla replied, "Your dad had the knack for ruining a lot of lives."

Dexter nodded slightly. They were both silent as the waitress delivered the food. After the waitress left, he said, "I heard what he did to you. I'm real sorry."

Charla sipped her tea.

Dexter said, "Well, maybe I'll get out of Port Huron now. This place drives me nuts. You know, Mom actually suggested that I should have gone to the band concert at Pine Grove Park yesterday. That's her idea of great entertainment."

"I went. It wasn't too bad."

"Ha. I told Mom that if she thought I was going to sit in the hot sun and listen to a bunch of local yokels fake their way through some stupid Sousa marches, she didn't know much."

Charla asked, "So what did you do?"

"Sat around and had some beers. I'm planning to go back to Detroit as soon as things are settled. Maybe I'll run Dad's business."

After they finished their meal, Dexter reached across the table and touched Charla's hand. Charla flinched and then willed herself to relax.

He looked at her beautiful blue eyes, lovely complexion, and full lips. He said, "I still care for you. Maybe things could be different for us now. Maybe we were meant to run into each other today. Maybe it's not too late for us."

She looked at his pasty complexion, watery eyes, and stubby fingers. *Maybe? Maybe never*, she thought. *I don't see how I ever thought this worm could make me happy.* She said, "We're both going through a rough time. For now, why don't we agree to keep in touch and be there for each other? Then we'll see what happens."

He squeezed her hand. "It's a promise."

Charla stood up, kissed Dexter on the cheek, and left the tavern, thinking about what she was going to do that night.

Dexter rubbed his cheek, leaned back, and ordered another beer.

*   *   *   *

When Toby boarded the trolley for his return trip to the police station, he heard a quiet but definite call of nature. By the time he reached his destination, the call had become an ear-deafening roar.

Toby scurried into the restroom and encased himself in one of the stalls. He was pleased to realize that not only had his zipper stayed in place, but it also saved him precious time in an emergency such as this.

He was almost finished when he heard two familiar voices enter the restroom talking about the weather. The two men, Sergeant Caleb Williams and Patrolman Wilbur Greene, were as different as night and day. Sergeant Williams was six foot two and weighed well over two hundred pounds. He was also one of the kindest men Toby knew. He was hesitant to say anything bad about people, even the ones he had to arrest. In contrast, Patrolman Greene was short, wiry, and had a face that resembled a ferret. He was suspicious of other people's motives and had a meanness that caused Toby to be wary around him.

The two men faced the urinals. Greene said, "Have you heard anything about the murder investigation?"

"No. Gressley and Toby left the station this morning and I haven't seen them since."

"It's a damn shame that Toby Sharpe got to be Gressley's errand boy. There are other people on the force with more experience."

Williams said, "Toby seems competent enough."

"Yeah, but me and some other guys on the force have been here longer."

"That's true but don't hold a grudge against Toby. It was Gressley's decision."

Greene said, "That Gressley's a know-it-all. He thinks he's better than the rest of us, just because he worked in Lansing."

"I don't think that's true. He's just kind of reserved."

"Reserved my eye. And I still don't like that Toby got the assignment. He probably buttered Gressley up in order to get picked."

Williams said, "Maybe you ought to talk to the chief or Gressley."

"Yeah. A lot of good that would do."

The two policemen flushed the urinals, washed their hands, and left the restroom. Toby sat thinking about what he had just heard. Greene had talked to him about other members of the police department, so Toby knew what kind of person he was. But it still hurt to hear himself described in such negative terms. He wondered how many other people thought the same way about his assignment and wondered if he should talk to anyone. For now, Toby decided to keep silent and keep working as hard as possible.

Toby left the restroom and entered Detective Gressley's office. He took a seat next to Sylvia and sighed. Sylvia asked, "What's wrong?"

"Oh, nothing's wrong. I was just thinking about something."

Gressley lit a cigarette and asked, "Any news from the coroner?"

Sylvia sat her coffee cup down. "He called about an hour ago. He said that the knife wounds were definitely the cause of death. The main artery in the neck was severed, which would have caused a tremendous loss of blood in a short period of time. He also said that the knife that killed Conroy had some kind of curved blade, like a dagger. He'll be sending a complete written report tomorrow."

Gressley asked, "Do we know that the body is actually Dexter Conroy?"

Sylvia said, "Yes. Mrs. Conroy and her son identified the body at the coroner's office earlier this morning. They saw the description in the paper this morning. I just finished talking to Mrs. Conroy. I've made an appointment for you to interview her and Dexter Jr. at five o'clock this afternoon."

Still talking to Sylvia, Gressley asked, "Did you find out anything about Conroy?"

"He owned a business in Detroit called Conroy Enterprises. His secretary was a little hesitant to talk at first. But she became quite chatty when she realized we shared a common political belief."

Gressley gave a wry smile. "It wouldn't by any chance be that women should have the right to vote?"

Sylvia grinned broadly. "As I said, she was willing to share as much as she knew about Conroy's private life, which sounds like a real mess. For one thing, he had started divorce proceedings, although his wife apparently isn't aware of how far things had progressed. The secretary called his wife to tell her that he would be coming to Port Huron and wanted to discuss the divorce issue Sunday. He also made it clear he didn't want to be seen in public with either his wife or their son. But the coroner said that Mrs. Conroy told him that she didn't know her husband was in town."

Toby asked, "Why would she lie about that?"

Sylvia said, "Maybe it was because Mr. Conroy was accusing her of being a habitual drunk."

Toby said, "I didn't know that was a reason for divorce."

Sylvia said, "I called Arthur Bagwell's law office and found out that it's one of six grounds for divorce in Michigan. The others are adultery, some kinds of physical disabilities, imprisonment, desertion for at least two years, or if you obtained a divorce in another state."

"A second thing I found out was that he was having an affair with a young thing by the name of Charlotte Clemons or Clements. But something happened about two weeks ago that threw a damper on the relationship."

Gressley asked, "Any idea what happened?"

"Maude didn't know. But the woman must have a temper because she went to the office and threw a vase at Conroy."

Gressley asked, "What did Charlotte look like?"

"She's tall, mid-twenties, blue eyes, and dark hair. Maude thought she was attractive, but hard-looking for someone her age."

Toby said, "That sounds like a woman who was leaving the Prince Albert Hotel this morning when I went over to check Conroy's room. The desk clerk said she was a prostitute who goes by the name of Charla."

Gressley said, "She's someone we need to find. Did Maude have any more information?"

"She said that Conroy's son was in trouble over huge gambling debts. Conroy Sr. was disgusted and said he wasn't going to help again."

Toby asked, "Who does he owe money to?"

"It was some funny-sounding name." Sylvia flipped through her notebook. "Here it is. His name is Slick Finley."

Gressley said, "That might sound like a funny name, but Slick is not a funny person. He's known around the state for using violence to get people to pay their debts."

Toby said, "Do you think he might have killed Conroy?"

Gressley said, "I doubt it. But it might have made Jr. angrier at his dad, and he could have lost his temper if his dad wouldn't give him the money."

Sylvia said, "The last thing I found out was that Conroy was involved in some kind of hush-hush business deal. It was so secret that even his secretary doesn't know any of the details."

Gressley asked, "Did any of this business discussion take place over the phone?"

"Yes. Maude said the calls came from Lansing but doesn't know who it was."

Toby was impressed with all the information Sylvia was able to obtain. He asked, "You learned all of this just because the two of you want the right to vote?"

"Think what I might have learned if I told her women ought to be on the regular police force."

Toby wondered if she was serious. Gressley knew she was.

Gressley turned to Toby. "Tobias, what were you able to find out?"

Toby said, "Conroy's room at the Prince Albert Hotel was broken into. I think someone came in through the window. Clarence and I were able to get some fingerprints off the windowsill."

Gressley asked, "When will he have the pictures ready?"

"He promised to deliver them to the station by four o'clock this afternoon. I then followed up on the phone call Sylvia got about a missing rowboat. I couldn't find any clues on the rowboat, but I did learn that the Conroys own a home in that area. I talked to some of their neighbors and got about the same information Sylvia did about the family."

Gressley asked, "What did you learn from Mr. Kimball?"

"He heard some voices Saturday night, but they were too far away to tell anything. He got up to check but didn't see anything. He did remember a rowboat on the beach about a block from the lighthouse that night, but it was not there Sunday morning."

Gressley said, "Good job." He then shared what he had learned on the *Tashmoo*. "Conroy got into an argument with someone who was rather short, with red hair, freckles, and a large Adam's apple. It also appears like someone might have broken into his suitcase. I was also told that Conroy was going to watch some races at Driving Park. I want to stop there on the way to the Conroys and see if anyone remembers him being there."

Sylvia asked, "Did anyone know the red-haired man's name?"

Gressley said, "No. But they did remember him getting off in Port Huron."

Toby said, "We have the names of two suspects: Mrs. Conroy and Dexter Jr."

Gressley said, "Yes. Then we need to locate the two mystery people: Charlotte and the man who was on the *Tashmoo*." Gressley turned back to Sylvia. "Tobias and I are going to be out the rest of the afternoon."

Sylvia gave Gressley a salute and left the room.

Gressley said, "Tobias, do you know how to drive a car?"

"Yes."

"Good. Chief Chambers informed me that he rented a car—a Ford Runabout, I believe—to be used for our investigative purposes. The department doesn't own cars but is willing to rent them for special purposes."

"You mean I won't be riding the trolley anymore?"

"That's right. And since I don't know how to drive, you'll be my chauffeur. We're going to Driving Park and then to visit Mrs. Conroy and her son."

As soon as Toby was outside, he saw the car sitting in front of the building. Feeling like a child at Christmas, Toby ran his hand along the fender of the Runabout. It was a two-seater with four cylinders and a 20-horsepower motor. Toby started the car and shifted into first gear. After gathering some speed, he shifted to top, or second, gear. "Nicely done," said Gressley. "So, I understand you're thinking of buying one of these contraptions for your family."

Toby said, "We're thinking about buying a Ford touring car sometime next year. It costs about $600 new, but it would seat the whole family. And there are good used ones available for about $300."

"I think motor cars are dangerous. Those gas lamps used for illumination could easily catch on fire. And if we hit anything going 30 miles an hour or faster, we would be catapulted out of these seats like a couple of roman candles on the fourth of July. Seems like they ought to at least come equipped with restraining belts."

"But they are fun to drive."

Gressley said, "From a law enforcement perspective, I think that's going to be one of the problems. Port Huron now has a population of over 20,000. In ten years there might be as many as four thousand cars in the city. Right now some-one doesn't even need any kind of permit to drive, and there are no tests for com-petency. I think cars are going to make our job more difficult."

"Well, at least we won't have to put up with as much horse manure in the city."

Gressley smiled. "I have to admit, the air does get a bit rancid on a hot sum-mer day. How much does a car like Bill Boyd's cost?"

"Almost $2,000."

"You're kidding! That's almost as much as a house. How can he afford to spend that much?"

"He inherited quite a lot of money. His mother died when he was born, and his dad died when he was about fifteen. That was about the time you moved to Port Huron. He had a difficult time with his father's death. His uncle, the owner of the *Star* newspaper, took care of him. He pretty much allows Bill to do what-ever he wants."

"Just a word of warning about your friend. Be careful what you say to him about the case. We don't want certain kinds of information getting in the newspaper."

After a few moments of silence, Toby said, "I've been thinking about Sylvia."

"What about her?"

"You seem to know her pretty well."

Gressley looked at Toby carefully. "What exactly do you mean?"

"Well, you've worked together for several years."

Gressley relaxed. "Yes, that's true. What's your question?"

"Was she serious about a woman being on the police force?"

"Oh, yes indeed. She thinks that a woman could be just as effective as a man."

Toby said, "I know she was really upset when the voters rejected the referendum on giving women the right to vote."

"What really made her angry was an ad in the *Times-Herald* that said, 'Ask your women folk whether they desire to lose their femininity. Ask the women; 90 percent do not want to vote.'"

"Women should have the right to vote, but I'm not sure about police work."

Gressley asked, "Why not?"

"Well, voting is mostly about thinking. You can read the paper, make a decision, and cast your vote. But police work can be physical. Can you imagine a woman running after and capturing a crook who outweighs her by fifty pounds?"

"You might have a point. But I think there are many areas of police work that women could do just as well as men."

"Like what?" Toby asked.

"I think a woman's investigative skills are just as good as a man's. And they would be good relating to the public."

Toby parked the car next to the entrance to Driving Park. The two men walked over to the gate. Gressley looked over the top. He yelled, "Anyone here?"

Within a few minutes, a large, white-haired man in a rumpled suit with a chaw of tobacco in his mouth walked over to the gate. "We ain't open on Mondays," he said.

Gressley said, "I'm Detective Gressley and this is Patrolman Sharpe. We understand that Mr. Conroy was here Saturday."

The white-haired man spat a stream of tobacco juice and wiped his chin. He then opened the gate to allow Gressley and Toby to enter. "Name's Chet, and I'm in charge of security. I don't know no Mr. Conroy."

Toby said, "He's about five foot six, weighed around 250 pounds, and had a moustache."

Chet asked, "Did he look like ex-President Taft?"

Gressley said, "So I understand."

"I remember him comin' for a few races. Then he got into an argument with a younger man. I got the idea that it was his son because they kinda looked alike. They were havin' such a rile that I had to separate them. When the younger man took a swing at me, I popped him a couple of times in the face. The kid folded like an accordion."

Gressley asked, "Do you remember anything they said?"

"Not much. At the end, I remember the older man saying that he was in town for some important business and didn't want to be seen with the kid while he was here."

Gressley said, "Thanks for your help."

When they returned to the car, Gressley pulled his pocket watch out of his vest. He said, "It's after four o'clock. Let's find out what Mrs. Conroy and her son have to say."

CHAPTER 13

▼

Detective Alexander stopped at his office to file a report and request a bulletin be sent to all Toronto police stations giving the descriptions of Nikki, Soma, and Zizi. He requested any information be sent to his office as soon as possible.

After completing his report, he drove to the Imperial Dance Hall. A man was standing behind the bar when Alexander entered the ballroom. He looked up as Alexander approached him.

He spoke sharply, "We don't open for another hour. If you're looking for a job, the manager is upstairs."

Alexander showed his badge. "I'm Detective Alexander, and may I ask who I'm addressing?"

"I'm Roscoe Ames, and I'm the chief bartender. What do you want?"

"Do know any of your customers named Soma Fekete, Zizi Balogh or a man called Nikki?" He proceeded to describe the two women.

Roscoe said, "I know Nikki real well. We call him the dance hall Don Juan. Seems like he's with a different girl every month. He's been spending a lot of time recently with someone who looks like the one you called Soma. I don't know her name, but I'm sure she has been here several times."

"Were any of them here Saturday night?"

"I don't think so."

Alexander said, "You said Nikki has a different girl every month. He must leave a lot of broken hearts."

"I guess so. I couldn't tell if he dumps the girls or if they dump him."

"What do you mean?"

"Well, they never come back, so I never get to ask," Roscoe said.

Alexander felt his throat tighten. "You mean they disappeared?"

"I never thought of it that way. I just figured they were so angry or hurt that they didn't want to see him again."

"How long has Nikki been coming here?"

Roscoe thought for a moment. "The first time I remember him was about six or seven months ago. Right around Christmas."

"And as far as you know, the girls he charmed never returned?"

"Nope."

Alexander slammed his notebook shut and stuffed it into his jacket. He handed Roscoe a business card. "If you see Nikki or either of the girls, please call me at this number."

Roscoe nodded. "Sure."

Alexander dashed out of the building and jumped into his car. As he drove back to his office, he concentrated on how he would write a bulletin that indicated Nikki was wanted for suspected kidnapping or murder.

*   *   *   *

Toby slowed down as they approached Lakeside Park. Gressley said, "When we get to the Conroys, I'll do most of the talking. But I want you to pay close attention to their responses and mannerisms. I also want you to look around the house for anything that suggests something about the family. We need to respect their loss, but they are also suspects."

As they pulled into the drive, they saw a brand-new canary yellow Pierce-Arrow. Gressley said, "I'd wager that costs a pretty penny."

"That's for sure," said Toby, admiring the sleek design and the plush leather interior.

Mrs. Conroy opened the front door. She was wearing a black dress of a finely woven fabric, with a hand-embroidered pattern in dark brown. She also wore an exquisite pearl necklace. She invited them in. Mrs. Conroy was a large woman. Toby guessed that she was nearly five foot nine and weighed about 170 pounds. After making introductions and accepting condolences, Mrs. Conroy led the two policemen into the living room. She introduced her son.

Dexter remained seated and gave a sullen nod to the policemen. He massaged a bruise on his left cheek.

Embarrassed by her son's response, Mrs. Conroy nervously took a sip from the opaque drinking glass she was holding. Toby wondered if it was gin or water in that glass.

Gressley said, "Your house is very nice. You have a wonderful view of the lake."

"Thank you. I certainly enjoy the time I spend here," replied Mrs. Conroy.

"Do you enjoy gardening? I noticed the beautiful English roses."

"Gardening is my favorite hobby."

Gressley could see several food dishes on the kitchen table. "Have the neighbors been sending food?"

"Yes. They've been very thoughtful. I think they were assuming the funeral would be in a couple of days. But I decided to have a memorial service in Detroit next month. That's where his friends and family live."

"That's understandable."

Mrs. Conroy said, "I've made some coffee. Would you like some?"

"Coffee would be fine, thanks," Gressley said.

"Son?"

"Yeah, me too."

Toby noticed that Dexter Jr. was about the same height and age as himself but somewhat flabby. *Give him another twenty years and he'll look just like his dad*, Toby thought.

Mrs. Conroy returned to the room with a large tray, which she sat on the coffee table. A slight tremor in her hands caused some of the coffee to spill. "I forgot to ask if you wanted cream or sugar, so I brought both. Please help yourselves."

The two policemen filled their cups. Toby noticed that instead of pouring coffee for herself, Mrs. Conroy continued to hold the glass she had when they arrived. She had apparently refilled it while she was in the kitchen.

Gressley said, "I know this is difficult, but we must ask you some questions that need to be asked concerning the nature of Mr. Conroy's death. I believe it would be easier if we interviewed each of you separately."

Mrs. Conroy nodded. "Of course."

Gressley looked at Dexter Jr. "If you don't mind Dexter, we would like to interview your mother first."

Dexter grunted, stood up, and sauntered to the door. He allowed it to bang loudly as he went outside.

Gressley turned to Mrs. Conroy. "Were you home Saturday night?"

"Yes. I read until about ten o'clock and then went to bed."

"Was Dexter Jr. home with you?"

"He was out when I went to bed. I'm not sure when he came home."

"I understand from the coroner that you were surprised that your husband was in town."

"Yes. I had no idea he was here."

"But we've been told by his secretary that she called you on Friday, saying that he wanted to discuss divorce proceedings with you."

Mrs. Conroy looked at her glass and then took a slow, long drink. "I…I…I'm just so embarrassed. I tried to be whatever he wanted, but it was never good enough. Then, about a month ago, he told me he wanted a divorce so he could remarry."

"What was the reason he was going to give for a divorce?"

Mrs. Conroy continued to stare at the glass in her hand. "I suppose you already know that too. He was going to claim that I'm a habitual drunk."

"How did you respond when he told you that?"

Mrs. Conroy said, "I became very angry. Wouldn't you? I know I drink too much at times. But so do a lot of other people, and they're not called habitual drunks."

Gressley asked, "Do you know the name of the woman your husband was planning to marry?"

"No. The only thing he said is that they have 'been seeing each other' for about a year."

"And you never tried to find out who she was?"

"No. He's been having affairs for years, but they never got this serious."

"We found out this morning that someone broke into your husband's room at the Prince Albert Hotel. It appeared that they were looking for something. Do you have any idea what it might have been?"

"Maybe it had something to do with his business. He was always involved in secret deals."

"Do you know what he was working on recently?"

Mrs. Conroy rubbed the pearl necklace. "No. I don't pay much attention to his business anymore."

"Do you know anyone who would want to harm your husband?"

"I know he's made business enemies, but I don't think any of them would resort to murder."

Gressley turned to Toby. "Patrolman Sharpe, please tell Dexter we want to talk to him now."

Toby, who had been quietly looking around the room, turned to Mrs. Conroy. "I was admiring the photographs on the mantle. Is that one your wedding picture?"

"Yes. We were married in 1888."

"You made a very handsome couple."

Mrs. Conroy smiled for the first time during their visit and left the room. Toby went to retrieve Dexter.

Dexter returned and slouched down in the sofa.

"Where were you last night?" Gressley asked.

"I was at the Marion Hotel until about midnight."

"Can anyone vouch for the time you left?"

"Sure. I was with three other people, drinking. But, now that I think about it, I actually left the hotel at about eleven. Then I just drove around for a while."

"Alone?"

"Yeah."

"How did you get that bruise on your cheek?"

Dexter rubbed his face. He did not respond.

"Would it refresh your memory if I told you we talked to a man named Chet at Driving Park just a few hours ago?"

"Yeah. I was talking to my dad for a few minutes. This guy came up and hit me."

"I understand that you and your dad didn't get along."

"That's an understatement."

"Why was that?"

"All he was interested in was making money and keeping as much of it as he could. He had no regard for anyone except himself."

"Like not wanting to cover your gambling debts?"

Dexter glared at Gressley for a moment. "Yeah. So what if I'm having a little bad luck right now? He owes me."

"I suppose Slick Finley was applying a lot of pressure," Gressley said.

Dexter shrugged his shoulders. "Yeah. Dad just didn't understand."

"Do you know the name of the woman your father was seeing?"

Dexter looked out the window before he answered. "No. I don't have any idea who she is."

"Do you know anything about your father's business deals?"

"No."

Gressley said, "Patrolman Sharpe, please bring Mrs. Conroy back."

When Toby and Mrs. Conroy returned, Gressley said, "We have the fingerprints found in Mr. Conroy's room at the Prince Albert Hotel. I would appreciate it if you would let Patrolman Sharpe take your fingerprints so we can compare them to ones we took this morning."

"You think we broke into Dad's room?" Dexter said. "That's crazy."

"If your fingerprints don't match, it would be a way to prove your innocence."

After a few minutes of hesitation, Mrs. Conroy said, "Detective Gressley's right. If we don't do it, we'll look guilty."

Toby retrieved his fingerprint equipment. "Just roll your finger on the ink pad and then roll it on this card."

When the fingerprinting was completed, Gressley said, "We appreciate your cooperation at this difficult time."

Mrs. Conroy set her glass down and walked Gressley to the door. Toby stopped, picked up the glass, and smelled the contents.

"You don't need to do that," said Dexter. "She's been drunk for about three years."

Once in the car, Toby said, "I guess we still have them on our list of suspects."

Gressley said, "Yes. They both have motive and neither one has a convincing alibi."

"But do you think a woman could actually kill someone in such a violent way? Men are much more likely to commit murders, especially if it is done with a knife or gun."

"It's true that women don't kill as often as men," Gressley said. "And it's conventional wisdom to think they would use a less violent means, like poison. But you have to accept the possibility that a woman, under the right conditions, could resort to violence. Remember what Carrie Nation was doing just a few years ago? She got arrested over thirty times for using her hatchet to destroy saloons."

Toby sped up to pass a horse-drawn ice wagon. "That's true. But at six feet, she was bigger than most men. And she had to be a little crazy."

Gressley said, "So tell me your observations of Mrs. Conroy—physically and mentally."

"I see what you're suggesting. She's a pretty big woman, she drinks too much, and neighbors say she was under quite a strain. But I still can't believe a woman could commit such a crime."

"You might be right. But as an investigator, you can't ignore the fact that she might have done it. Same with her son. And then, we still have two other suspects to track down. The wisest thing to do right now is to collect more evidence instead of developing theories about who is more likely to commit murder."

Toby parked the Model T in front of the police station. As they got out of the car, Gressley asked, "How did you like using a car to do our job?"

"I liked it a lot. But I was thinking that a four-passenger car would be better. What if we had to transport someone?"

"That's a good idea. I'll talk to Chief Chambers about it. Maybe someday the city will purchase a car just for the police department. For now, you might as well keep this car at your house. Just don't use it too often for your personal travel."

"I'll be sure to take good care of it."

They entered the police station. Gressley asked, "Did Smith's Photography send over the photos you took of the fingerprints at the Prince Albert Hotel this morning? If they're here, they would be in the top drawer of that filing cabinet in the corner."

Toby took a folder from the filing cabinet and handed it to Gressley.

"Good," Gressley said. "Now let's see what we've got." Gressley compared the fingerprints taken at the Conroys with the photos, then slid them over to Toby. "What do you think?"

Toby said, "I don't think they look very similar."

"I agree. It doesn't look like either Dexter Jr. or his mother broke into Mr. Conroy's room."

Gressley put the folder away and then said, "Let's call it a day. You go home to your family. I'll see you eight o'clock sharp tomorrow morning."

CHAPTER 14

▼

Sylvia Pointe undid her corset and hurled it across the room. *Holy Helen of Troy,* she thought. *Why do I wear this thing?* The offending undergarment perched precariously on the edge of the bed. Then, like a retreating snake, it slithered silently to the floor.

She stood in the middle of her bedroom, looking in the mirror. She was in her mid-thirties, and her body still maintained its firmness. Her sandy-colored hair was bobbed short, an appropriate style for its natural wave.

Sylvia had always been physically active. As a young girl, she could outrun and outclimb most of the boys her age. Currently, her main exercise was confined to weekend bicycling. Her adventurous tomboy nature as a teenager concerned her parents and discouraged some males from dating her. But it was a major contributing factor to her marriage.

Jake Pointe was romantic, impetuous, and handsome. After a short romance, they married in 1897 when Sylvia was eighteen. The first year of marriage was unbelievably wonderful. Then came the Spanish-American War.

As soon as Jake heard of the sinking of the *Maine,* he rushed to enlist. His idealism led him to believe that he would either not be killed or that he would die heroically. However, that was not to be. Within two weeks after arriving in Cuba, he contracted yellow fever. He suffered terribly from chills, swollen joints, headaches, and delirium. He died a month later. Thus, without seeing a battlefield or firing a single bullet, Jake Pointe became a casualty of the war.

Upon hearing of Jake's death, Sylvia went into a deep depression. For the next six months, she spent most of the time lying in her childhood bed in her parents' home. Gradually, however, the oppressive fog began to lift. As she regained her old vigor, she began to think about the future.

She was only twenty years old. Remarriage was an obvious option, but Sylvia would not consider it. She wanted to be independent, which meant she needed to get a job. Fortunately, she was able to find employment at the Port Huron police department as a secretary.

In addition to employment, Sylvia needed to plan her future. Her parents convinced her to talk to someone at the Ladies of the Maccabees of the World, an auxiliary body of the fraternal order known as the Knights of the Maccabees. LOTMOTW was organized in 1891, and had its main headquarters in Port Huron. The primary function was to provide its members with disability benefits or retirement benefits at age seventy. Starting from scratch, the organization had 150,000 members throughout the United States, Canada, and Great Britain in 1913.

When Sylvia talked to a representative, she was immediately impressed. She not only enrolled as a member but became involved in the organization's charitable programs. Sylvia remembered the thousands of dollars sent to San Francisco after the devastating earthquake of 1906. The willingness of members around the world to send what they could was a heartwarming activity.

As Sylvia slipped into a comfortable housedress, she thought about the impressive ways the Ladies of the Maccabees of the World helped women. It motivated her to keep pushing for women to be accepted as regulars on the police force. She had talked to the chief of police and the city mayor but to no avail. Women were hired as matrons at the jail, but Sylvia felt that policewomen on the streets would show that women are as capable as men in protecting the community. She hoped to be the first one but doubted it would ever happen.

She was thankful, however, that Detective John Gressley was including her in the current murder investigation. Her official title was recording secretary, so technically she was not doing police work. But she knew John respected her opinion, and she appreciated his willingness to give her this opportunity.

She and John had been seeing each other for about three years. It was interesting to Sylvia to observe the difference between John and Jake. She admired John's cautious, logical approach to life. Of course, what irritated her at times was his cautious, logical approach to life. She loved John but was reluctant to get married. For one thing, she was sure that the city would not permit a husband and wife to be employed in the same department. And after fifteen years of independence, she was leery of the ways in which marriage would change her life.

She walked to the kitchen and fixed a meal from the leftovers of Sunday's pot roast dinner. After eating, she stretched out on the sofa and began reading *The Window at the White Cat,* a mystery novel by Mary Roberts Rinehart. After a few minutes, her eyes closed, and she was fast asleep.

*   *   *   *

When Toby returned home, he saw Bill Boyd's car parked in front of his house. He smiled, thinking Mary must have invited him for supper. Toby knew Bill couldn't resist a home-cooked meal. Bill was sitting on the porch, playing with Chris. They gave Toby a wave as he rolled to a stop.

Toby asked, "Are you here for another free meal?"

Bill laughed. "I knew you would say that. So, with the help of your son, I'm going to sing for my supper." Bill and Chris embarked on an off-key rendition of Irving Berlin's *Alexander's Ragtime Band.*

When they finished, Toby applauded. He said, "That was very loud." Noticing the expectant look on his son's face, he quickly added, "And very good."

Mary walked out on the porch. She asked, "What's going on out here? It sounds like fun."

"Daddy's here," yelled Chris. "And he's got a motor car!"

Mary, with her daughter perched on one hip, walked to the gleaming black Ford Runabout.

Toby grinned broadly. "What do you think?"

Mary said, "It looks great, but why are you driving it?"

"Chief Chambers rented it for the investigation. Since Detective Gressley doesn't know how to drive, I have the honor. I get to keep it at home if I don't use it for personal reasons."

Jumping up and down, Chris shouted, "I want a ride. I want a ride."

"Well, I suppose once around the block won't hurt."

Chris immediately jumped into the passenger seat. Once they were underway, Chris pointed at the brake pedal. "What's that?"

"That's the brake. I use it when I want to stop the car."

Chris said, "I'm going to have a car when I grow up."

"You are?"

"Yes. It's going to be purple and have eight wheels."

As soon as they returned, Amanda cried, "Me ride, me ride."

Mary sat in the passenger seat and held Amanda on her lap. Frightened by her first ride in an automobile, Amanda, gripping her favorite doll, screamed the entire time.

Toby laughed. "Maybe I could take her along tomorrow if we need to warn people to get out of the way."

During dinner, Toby told a little bit about the day. He noticed that Chris had moved his chair a little closer during the meal. *Amazing how impressed a four-year-old is with a little car ride,* thought Toby.

Bill finished his second helping of potato salad. He said, "That was a delicious meal."

Mary said, "Thanks. It's Toby's grandmother's recipe. Would anyone like some ice cream?"

Everyone at the table yelled yes.

Mary and Toby went into the kitchen. Toby got the bowls out of the cupboard and stood beside Mary as she dipped the ice cream. Mary said, "Your mom's going to come over and watch the kids for a few hours tomorrow."

Toby nodded.

"We have an interview with the Life-Saving Service about putting guards at the St. Clair River Tunnel."

Toby nodded.

"Then Nancy and I are going to take all our clothes off and run around Pine Grove Park."

Toby nodded.

"Toby!"

"What? Oh. Sorry. It's just that Gressley told me to get a good night's rest, but I can't keep from thinking about that darn murder case."

"Why don't you ask Bill if he wants to go out for a few drinks? Maybe that would help you relax."

"Good idea."

When Toby and Mary returned from the kitchen, Toby looked at Bill. He asked, "How would you like to go to the Hotel Marion for a couple of beers after we're done with the ice cream? My treat."

"Would I? Is the Pope Catholic?"

*   *   *   *

Sylvia felt a light touch on her forehead, then on her nose. When she felt a slightly firmer touch on her leg, she opened her eyes and saw Gressley kneeling in front of her. She murmured quietly, "If you take me into the bedroom, I'll give you an hour to stop."

An hour later, they were relaxing in bed, enjoying a cigarette and a glass of wine, when Sylvia said, "What do you think of the controversy over white slavery?"

Gressley rolled over on his side and looked at her. Then he laughed. "Talk about a change of pace. Or was it something I did?"

Sylvia punched him lightly. "I've just been thinking about the speech Mrs. Cullenbine gave Saturday. So what's your opinion?"

"I think it's serious, but I also believe the numbers are exaggerated."

"Do you think it would do any good to monitor the tunnel, the way Mrs. Cullenbine suggested?"

"It seems like a waste of time to me, but you never know. Our police department certainly doesn't have the money to do it."

"But maybe some private citizen could do it."

"That might be dangerous. Somebody could wind up getting hurt."

Sylvia said, "I'm glad that movie *Traffic in Souls* was made. It really did a good job showing how easy it would be to kidnap someone."

"That's true. I understand it is being shown to the immigrants arriving at Ellis Island in New York as a warning of what might happen to them if they're not careful. But something that concerns me about movies is the way they could be used for propaganda."

"How do you mean?"

"Do you remember a book called *The Clansman* that was so popular in 1905?"

"Was that the one that glorified the Ku Klux Klan? I couldn't believe that it got as high as fourth on the bestseller list."

"That's the book," Gressley said. "A lot of people I know, including some policemen, accepted it as true. Now supposing someone made that into a movie. I think it would encourage people to join the Klan and could lead to more violence in our country."

"Do you think anyone in the Port Huron police department is a member of the Klan?"

"I don't know for sure. But if I had to pick a likely candidate, it would be Wilbur Greene. I've heard him say some pretty mean things about Negroes and Catholics."

Sylvia leaned over and kissed Gressley's chest. "Are you satisfied with today's investigation?"

"Yes. We got a lot done today, but it's important that we find out about the man from the *Tashmoo* and the girl Mr. Conroy was having an affair with as soon as possible."

"Do you think Mrs. Conroy or her son Dexter might have done it?"

"It's possible. They both had motive and opportunity and neither one has any kind of alibi. But I don't want to overlook other possibilities. We have so much to learn that it's impossible to speculate. Toby's having a hard time believing that a woman could commit murder."

"That's just like him. He was raised to believe that women are incapable of that kind of violence."

Gressley caressed Sylvia's shoulder. "What do you think?"

"I suppose we are all capable of murder. I have a hunch Mr. Conroy was killed by a woman."

"Why?"

Sylvia said, "Someone like his wife or his ex-girlfriend could have been so angry that once she started stabbing him, she couldn't stop. I know most murders are committed by men, but I believe some women can be just as violent. Remember Lizzie Borden, and the playground verse children were reciting a few years ago? 'Lizzie Borden took an axe and gave her mother forty whacks. And when she saw what she had done, she gave her father forty-one.'"

"But the jury found Lizzie Borden not guilty."

"What about Molly Pitcher during the Revolutionary War? She kept loading a cannon after her husband was shot even though the British came so close to shooting her that one musket ball went between her legs. She was heard to say that if the shot would have been a few inches higher, she would have lost her occupation."

Gressley said, "That showed that a woman can be just as brave as a man, but Molly Pitcher didn't murder anyone."

Sylvia pinched Gressley on the leg. "Don't be such a stick-in-the-mud. I'm just saying that if a woman gets angry enough, she can do anything a man can do."

Gressley raised his arms in mock surrender. "OK, OK. I get your point. But we don't know what kind of anger Conroy provoked in other people. I'll remind you of the same thing I told Toby. We have to keep our minds open and concentrate on gathering more evidence."

Sylvia said, "I understand what you're saying. I don't want it to be a woman. I just have a feeling that it is."

"Woman's intuition?"

"Something like that. How did Toby do today?"

Gressley said, "He did a good job as far as I could tell. I don't think he made any major blunders. I'm still a little concerned about his lack of experience."

"Oh, I don't think you need to worry." Sylvia placed the back of her hand on her forehead and closed her eyes. "My woman's intuition says he's at home now, drinking a glass of ginger ale, and reading *Mutt and Jeff*."

*   *   *   *

Soma and Zizi watched warily as Charlie and Carl entered the room. Charlie carried several boxes, and Carl held two buckets of water, soap, and towels. Charlie sat the boxes down and removed the gags from the women's mouths. He said, "We're about ready to leave."

Zizi asked, "What do you mean?"

Charlie smiled. "Oh, I think you remember what we talked about yesterday. We're going to go to the United States. Carl and I don't want you looking like a couple of ragamuffins, so we bought you some new clothes."

Carl began untying the ropes that bound the women's hands and feet. "And we don't want you smellin' like a couple of foreign skunks, so you're goin' to wash before you get dressed." Carl finished untying the ropes. "Now take your clothes off and start washing."

Soma held her arms across her breasts. She looked at Carl. "I am not taking my clothes off in front of you!"

Carl grabbed her arms and jerked them away from her body. "I don't think you have a choice." He grinned lewdly. "It's about time I get to see what's inside that shirt."

Zizi yelled, "Leave her alone!" She shrieked loudly, "Help! Anyone! Help!"

Soma slapped Carl across the face and joined Zizi in yelling for help.

Charlie and Carl quickly subdued and gagged the women. Charlie looked into Soma's eyes. "I know this is embarrassing, but it has to be done. I want each of you to go to a different corner of the room, wash yourselves real good, and change clothes." He held Soma's arm gently. "I'll make sure Carl doesn't bother you."

Soma nodded, picked up the soap and water, and walked slowly to one corner of the room. Zizi stared angrily at the two men for a few moments before she picked up her bucket, and went to another corner.

Charlie turned to Carl. "Go hitch up the horse. Somebody might have heard them yelling. As soon as they're cleaned and dressed, we'll get out of here."

CHAPTER 15

▼

Luke Laboy watched the two men get out of Bill Boyd's car and walk into the hotel. He recognized the stocky man with curly hair as the policeman he saw earlier at the Prince Albert Hotel. The knowledge that a policeman would be in the hotel when he committed his crime made Luke feel more excited. He waited until the two men were inside and then scurried around to the side of the building. He placed a box under the window of Edgar Reynolds' room. *This is going to be easier than the Prince Albert because the windows aren't so high,* he thought. He broke the window, cleaned away the shards of glass, and pulled himself through the opening.

*   *   *   *

As they entered the lobby, the desk clerk at the Hotel Marion said, "Good evenin', Mr. Boyd."

"Hi, Ronnie. How are you doing? My friend and I are here for a couple of beers." They walked through the lobby into the bar.

When the waiter came to the table, Toby ordered two Cream of America beers. After the waiter left, Bill rubbed his hands together. "Now tell me all the juicy parts of your investigation."

"You know I can't do that. Gressley would have my hide."

Both sat quietly for a moment. Bill shrugged his shoulders, and said, "OK, how about a safe topic? What do you think of the Tigers this year?"

"That I can talk about. With Cobb and Crawford on the team, their offense ought to be pretty good."

"But their pitching stinks. They're in sixth place now, and I don't see them doing much better."

"Yeah, I wish they had someone like Walter Johnson or Eddie Cicotte."

Bill asked, "What do you think of Cobb's salary demands?"

"Fifteen thousand dollars for playing ball? I think it's too much."

"But it makes sense from an economic standpoint. After all, who do the fans come to see?"

"What did he finally settle for?"

"Twelve thousand. But Navin's going to prorate it for the two weeks he missed. So the cheapskate is paying him $11,332.55! Can you believe it?"

Toby abruptly stopped the conversation and said, "Turn around slowly and look at the redheaded man in the restaurant."

Bill looked in the direction Toby indicated. "That's Edgar Reynolds. Why?"

"How do you know him?"

"I saw him here at the Marion today. He's the state official I did an interview with Sunday. He's in town to talk about road construction with city and county officials."

"He looks like a guy we're trying to find. Someone who resembles him was on the *Tashmoo* with Mr. Conroy."

"Why don't I ask Ronnie when he checked in?"

"You can't do that."

"Better me than you. If he sees you tomorrow, he might make a connection. Besides, Ronnie owes me a favor. I kept some embarrassing information out of the paper—figured he was a decent kid and needed a break."

"What was it?"

"Best you don't know, Patrolman Sharpe."

"Oh, jeez. OK, but don't do anything else."

"Trust me."

*   *   *   *

After Luke entered the room, he walked over and unlocked the door. *This is easy*, he thought. He remembered Pastor Bryan saying that everyone had a calling. *Looks like this is mine*, he thought. *Charla only wanted me to unlock the door, but I might as well see if there's anything worth taking.* He looked at the closet. *Nothing here.* When he rifled through the dresser, he found Reynolds' camera. Luke put the leather strap around his neck.

*　　　*　　　*　　　*

Bill approached the desk. "Ronnie, I wonder if you could tell me when Mr. Reynolds checked in."

"Sure can. I checked him in myself at about three o'clock Saturday. He came in on the *Tashmoo.*"

Bill folded a sheet of paper and placed a five-dollar bill inside. He slid it over to Ronnie. "How about telling me what his room number is and giving me the master key for about ten minutes."

Ronnie whispered, "I can't do that. I'll get fired."

"No one will ever know. I just thought this would make us even."

Ronnie's eyes narrowed. "That sounds almost like blackmail." But he wrote down the room number and slipped Bill the key. "Ten minutes—no longer."

Bill bounded up the stairs, taking two steps at a time, hurrying by a young woman who had just entered the lobby.

Oh no, thought Toby. *Where in thunder is he going?* He walked over to the desk. "Hi, Ronnie. Did Bill go up to Reynolds' room?"

"Who are you?"

"I'm his best friend, and I'm trying to keep him out of trouble."

Ronnie turned to look at the clock behind him. "Yeah, he went to Mr. Reynolds' room, and he's only got six minutes before I go get him."

Toby found a seat in the lobby across from the desk. He positioned himself so he could see the stairs yet keep an eye on Mr. Reynolds in case he left the restaurant.

*　　　*　　　*　　　*

Luke took one last look around the room. *If I'm going to be a professional thief,* he thought, *I ought to leave a calling card.* He took out his pocketknife and slashed his initials in the chair's upholstery. He was easing himself out of the window when he saw the doorknob begin to turn.

Bill turned the doorknob of room 210. *That's funny,* he thought. *It's already unlocked.* He opened the door and immediately noticed the broken window. Without closing the door, he hurried over to the window and looked out. He was unable to see anything. Bill turned to look at the room. He had no idea what he was looking for, but thought it might be interesting to see if Mr. Reynolds was hiding something. He did not find anything interesting under the bed or in the closet.

Bill looked at the chair's torn fabric. It looked like the number seventy-seven or the letters LL. He got down on his knees and looked under the chair. *Ah ha*, he thought. *What's this?* He reached for an envelope taped to the bottom of the chair. Then he inhaled the fragrance of perfume. Bill looked up. But before he could see anyone, he was greeted with a blow to the head, followed by a cascade of bright lights and then darkness.

*   *   *   *

Toby watched the young woman walk down the stairs. He thought she looked familiar. Their eyes locked for a moment before the woman headed for the exit. Toby turned his head to check on Mr. Reynolds who was no longer seated at his table. Toby rose and walked quickly to the restaurant door, where he saw Mr. Reynolds enter the restroom.

Toby was about to sit down when it struck him who he had seen leaving the hotel. Charla! He ran out the door and looked in all directions. She was nowhere in sight. He returned to the lobby where Ronnie was helping a dazed Bill Boyd down the stairs. Ronnie said, "You'd better get some ice for your friend's head."

Bill said, "Someone was in Reynolds' room. It was all messed up."

As Toby helped Bill out the door, Ronnie said, "Don't ask for any more favors, Mr. Boyd. I've paid my debt."

Toby turned to Ronnie. "I'm Patrolman Sharpe of the Port Huron police. Don't let anyone into Reynolds' room until I get back. Reynolds is in the restaurant. Tell him someone broke into his room. If he wants to get into his room, don't let him. Explain that you contacted the police, and they want to examine it first. Give him another room for the night. I'll be back in about thirty minutes. And whatever you do, don't tell him about Bill going into his room."

Toby pushed Bill into the passenger side of Bill's car. "I'm driving," he said. After Toby seated himself behind the wheel, he asked, "What the devil were you thinking?"

Rubbing the back of his head, Bill said, "I just had this bright idea that I might be able to find something interesting, and I did. There was an envelope under the chair. I was bending over to get it when someone hit me. When I came to, the envelope was missing."

"But don't you understand that this is a murder investigation? You're always doing zany things, but this was the dumbest. Did you wear gloves?"

Bill mumbled, "No."

Toby raced the car's motor. "Great! I guess we know whose prints will be on the doorknob."

Across the street from the hotel, Charla remained hidden behind a large oak tree until the car with the two men left. She was thankful she recognized the young policeman before he remembered who she was. Charla walked quickly to the boardinghouse, clutching the envelope she had taken from Mr. Reynolds' room.

*   *   *   *

Toby drove to his house. On the way, Bill told him about the broken window and the slashed upholstery. Toby stopped the car and ran in the house to get some ice and his detective kit. He returned to Bill's car and gave him the ice.

"Are you sure you can drive home?"

Bill nodded and drove away.

Toby jumped in the Runabout and headed for Smith's Photography. Clarence Smith was just finishing in the darkroom when Toby knocked on the door. Clarence opened the door and invited him in.

"I know it's late, but could you help me? There has been another break-in. This time it was at the Hotel Marion, and it looks similar to what happened at the Prince Albert Hotel. Could you come and photograph the fingerprints?"

"Of course. Let me get my equipment."

They got in the car and headed for the Hotel Marion. Clarence asked, "Detective Gressley thinks fingerprinting is going to become an important aspect of criminal investigation, doesn't he?"

"Yes. That's why I thought to bring you tonight."

"I'm happy to help. But you might want to learn how do this yourself. I'd be willing to give you some lessons."

Toby asked, "Doesn't that take a lot of skill?"

"Yes. But it would make you more valuable to the police department. Besides, it won't be long before Eastman Kodak will be selling fingerprinting cameras to law enforcement agencies."

When Toby and Clarence entered the hotel's lobby, Reynolds was arguing with Ronnie. Toby hurried over to where they were standing. He said, "I understand that a room has been broken into."

Reynolds, his face flushed, shouted, "Who the hell are you?"

"I'm Tobias Sharpe of the Port Huron police department and this is Clarence Smith. We're responding to a breaking and entering call." Looking at Reynolds, he asked, "Who are you?"

"I'm Edgar Reynolds, and it's my room that was broken into."

Toby nodded.

Edgar asked, "What kind of town is this? I was attacked publicly yesterday. And now someone breaks into my room."

Toby led the group upstairs to the room. When Reynolds began to enter, Toby placed his hand firmly on his shoulder. He said, "I'm sorry, but I can't let anyone else in the room until we have a chance to examine it. Then you can see if anything is missing."

Toby and Clarence entered the room. Toby said, "I'll dust for prints on the windowsill and doorknob so you can take some pictures." He looked at broken pieces of what used to be some kind of ceramic object and thought that was what was used on Bill's head.

After Toby completed his investigation, he told Reynolds he could come in.

Reynolds entered the room. He looked nervously at the overturned chair. "What a mess," he said.

Toby asked, "Do you see anything missing?"

Reynolds looked into the closet and the dresser. "Someone stole my camera."

"Anything else?"

"No."

Toby asked, "Do you have any idea what these pieces of ceramic are?"

"There was an ugly flower vase on the table near the door. I suppose that's what it is."

Toby pointed to the overturned chair. "What about that chair? Did it have those rips in it when you checked into the hotel?"

Reynolds gave Toby a disgusted look. "Do you think I would have stayed in the room if it had been like this? The intruder must have done it."

Toby leaned down and pulled a strip of tape from the chair. A piece of paper was attached to the tape. Toby said, "It looks like a part of an envelope is stuck to this tape. Any idea what it might be?"

Reynolds bit his lip. "No. It's probably been there a long time."

Toby said, "When we were in the lobby, you mentioned something about being attacked yesterday. What was that about?"

"I was minding my own business in Pine Grove Park, when this young hooligan ran past and threw a bucket of water on me. I gave chase but couldn't catch him."

"What did he look like?"

"I didn't get a good look at his face. He was short and wore his knickerbockers below the knees."

"Do you have any idea why he did it?"

"I have absolutely no reason why he picked on me."

Toby looked at Ronnie. "That's all for now. Will you be able to give Mr. Reynolds another room for the night?"

Ronnie nodded. "Yes, sir. I can put Mr. Reynolds in another room two doors down."

Reynolds said, "One more night in this town is all I can take."

Toby drove to Smith's Photography. As Clarence was getting out of the car, Toby asked, "Would it be possible to pick the pictures up at seven-thirty tomorrow morning?"

Mr. Smith said, "They'll be ready. I'll start developing them right now. And don't forget. The offer still stands on teaching you how to use my fingerprint camera."

"I appreciate your help, and I'll think about your offer." Toby returned to his car and drove home.

*   *   *   *

Charla entered her room, turned on the lights, and removed her gloves. She opened the envelope and allowed the contents to fall on the bed. She arranged the six photos in a straight line. Then she ran her long, well-manicured fingers around the edge of each photo. They were pictures of a naked fifteen-year-old girl in seductive poses. She walked over to the desk, picked up an ashtray and a book of matches, and placed them in the middle of the bed.

She held the first photo at one corner and lit the match. Catching fire, the ashes fell into the ashtray. As each photo burst into flames, images and voices flickered through her mind.

With the first photo, the best friend of her father is telling a fifteen-year-old girl it will be fun. "The pictures will just be for my personal collection," he said. "No one else will ever know."

With the second photo, she realizes that was false. Others will know because a sixteen-year-old girl is confronted by her father. "You little tramp. Get out of my house and never come back."

Third photo: A Port Huron madam welcomes an eighteen-year-old into her establishment. Things went fine for two years. Then she is told to leave because some of the customers had complained.

For the fourth photo, she remembers being on a train to Detroit. Dexter Conway Jr. begins a conversation with a twenty-year-old woman. He had known her in Port Huron and knew what she did for a living. But that didn't seem to matter. The next year was the happiest of her life as Dexter showered her with love and affection but not much money.

Fifth photo: A year later, she and Dexter are in a restaurant. Dexter's father comes over and joins them. The next day she gets flowers from the father. The son calls later to say they cannot see each other any more. Dexter Conway Sr. is not as romantic, but he is rich. Six months later, he proposes marriage. Dexter Jr. never calls again.

As she sets fire to the sixth photograph, she remembers that only two weeks ago Dexter Conroy Sr. slaps her hard. "What the hell are these?" He throws seven photos at her. "You think you can play me for a sucker?" She tries to explain that she was young and innocent when the pictures were taken. He yells, "You posed for seven pictures. You don't look innocent in any of them."

Seventh photo—Charla's reverie is suddenly interrupted. She grabs the envelope and looks inside. She screams, "Damn it! Where is the seventh picture?"

She slams the ashtray on the table and undresses. She suffers a tortured sleep, haunted by the ghosts of her past and thoughts about what happened to the missing photo.

*　　*　　*　　*

Across town, Toby lies awake wondering what he is going to tell Detective Gressley in the morning.

CHAPTER 16

▼

Residents of Toronto braced for a storm as ominous black clouds hovered over the city. The day began hot and muggy, but a northern cold front had dramatically lowered the temperature. Men and women held on to their hats as the blustery wind swirled past them. The ones who tried to open their umbrellas found that they were soon holding useless objects that had been turned inside out. The storm reached its zenith during the morning with dazzling bolts of lightening and explosive cracks of thunder. Then the hail began. Pieces of ice, the size of marbles, pelted the unfortunate few who had not taken cover.

The frightening sounds of the storm were amplified inside the freight train's boxcar, where Zizi and Soma lay bound and gagged. Charlie and Carl brought them aboard at dawn. The four were now waiting for the train to depart for Port Huron.

Zizi looked at Soma. She could not believe how much her friend had changed in less than forty hours. Soma's once adventurous spirit had been the primary reason they left Eastern Europe for Canada. Soma gave Zizi courage during the Atlantic voyage and during the early days in Toronto when they were unemployed.

Soma's transformation from a vigorous, energetic woman to her current state of listlessness reminded Zizi of a bright carnival balloon slowly deflating over a period of time.

Equally puzzling to Zizi had been Soma's relationship with Charlie. Beginning last night, every time Charlie came into their room, Soma's eyes would follow him. When Soma's gag was removed during dinner, she smiled and spoke to Charlie with respect. Zizi knew Soma well enough to understand that she was not flirting. It seemed to Zizi that Soma had surrendered, that somehow she had become dependent on Charlie.

Zizi realized that Soma seldom looked at her anymore. What little energy Soma had was directed toward Charlie. Zizi noticed that somehow Soma had moved physically closer to Charlie during the two hours since they were placed in the boxcar.

Zizi saw that when Charlie noticed Soma edging closer to him, he reacted with an odd expression. Zizi wondered if Charlie was feeling pity, disgust, or compassion. She hoped he felt guilty. Charlie stood up and walked to the other side of the boxcar. Zizi saw that when he moved away, Soma slowly curled into a fetal position.

The storm gradually subsided. But now Zizi was aware of a different sensation. The freight train jerked forward. For the first time since she was captured, Zizi cried.

*   *   *   *

The cold front that pummeled Toronto did not reach Port Huron, where it remained hot and humid. But Toby's thoughts were not about the weather as he stopped at Smith's Photography and picked up the pictures from the sleepy-eyed owner. As soon as he arrived at the station, Toby removed the Conroy murder file from the cabinet and compared the fingerprints taken from the Hotel Marion last night to the ones taken earlier at the Prince Albert Hotel. Even to Toby's inexperienced eye, they appeared to be a perfect match. He carried the folder into Detective Gressley's office.

Toby and Sylvia took their seats in front of Gressley's desk. Toby tapped his fingers on the folder wondering how he was going to explain what happened last night.

Gressley reached for his tin of Fatimas as he said, "Our main objective this morning is to see if we can locate two people: the man Conroy was talking to on the *Tashmoo* and Charlotte, the mystery woman. Tobias, do you have any ideas?"

"I think so."

"How's that?"

Toby nervously rubbed his hand across his mouth. "I think I might have seen both of them last night."

"Last night?"

"Well, I was really restless after dinner, so Bill Boyd and I went to the Hotel Marion for a couple of beers." He hesitated for a few seconds.

Gressley raised his eyebrows. "Go on."

"We saw someone who looked like the man from the *Tashmoo*. His name is Edgar Reynolds. He's from the Michigan State Highway Department, and he's in town talking to government officials from the counties in the Thumb area."

Gressley said, "I remember the article in yesterday's paper."

"Bill went to the hotel desk and got a key to Reynolds' room."

Gressley sat up straight in his chair. "Wait a minute. You allowed a civilian to break into somebody's room?"

"Well, sir, I didn't exactly allow him to do it. I thought he was just going to ask the man at the desk if he knew how the red-haired guy got to Port Huron. Anyway, when he went to the room, he found the door was unlocked. Someone had entered through the window, the same as at the Prince Albert Hotel. Bill saw an envelope taped under a chair. When he got down on his knees to get it, someone hit him over the head. The last thing he remembered before he got knocked out was the smell of perfume."

Gressley leaned forward. "Then what happened?"

"When he woke up, the envelope was gone. I think that Charlotte woman, who was going to marry Conroy, might have been the one who hit him. You know—the one who goes by the name of Charla. A woman that fits her description went up and down the stairs during the time Bill was in the room. Also, I'm sure I saw the same woman at the Prince Albert Hotel yesterday morning."

"Didn't you try to follow her?"

Toby squirmed in his seat. "I was concentrating on Reynolds so much that I didn't make a connection until it was too late. I ran outside, but she had already disappeared."

"What was Reynolds' room like?"

Toby pulled the pictures that he had taken the night before out of the folder and laid them on the table. "It was all messed up, like someone was looking for something."

Gressley pointed to one of the pictures. "What's all of those pieces on the floor?"

"Reynolds said it was a vase that was in the room. I think it was used to hit Bill over the head. I think the person who broke into Reynolds' room was the same one who entered Conroy's room at the Prince Albert Hotel."

"Do you have any evidence that supports that idea?"

Toby showed Gressley fingerprint photos. "I think so. I asked Clarence Smith to take pictures of the fingerprints on the windowsill and the doorknob. Some of them look the same."

Gressley took a magnifying glass and analyzed the prints carefully. He handed them back to Toby. "You're right. Except for the ones on the outside doorknob, some appear to be a match. Any idea about the ones on the outside doorknob?"

"I suppose those are Bill's."

"What are those markings on the chair in that other picture?"

Toby said, "Depending on how you look at the picture, it looks like it's either the number seventy-seven or the initials LL. I don't have any idea what it means."

Gressley handed the pictures back to Toby. "How did Reynolds behave last night?"

"Oh, he was really angry. In addition to his room, someone threw water on him in Pine Grove Park Sunday afternoon."

Gressley said, "I wonder if that was done so that Reynolds would go back to his room. That way the intruder could follow him in order to find out where he was staying. Did Reynolds say anything was missing from his room?"

"He said that the only thing missing was his camera, but Bill was convinced there was an envelope under the chair."

"Maybe Bill was mistaken."

Toby opened another folder. He said, "I found this piece of paper stuck to some tape under the chair. It looks like part of an envelope. Mr. Reynolds got real nervous when I asked him about it."

"It does look like someone was looking for the envelope," Gressley said. "I wonder what possible connection there is between Reynolds and Charla."

Gressley glanced at Sylvia and said, "Would you leave us alone for a while?"

Sylvia began to say something, thought better of it, and quietly closed the door as she left the room.

Gressley stared at Toby for a few seconds. When he spoke, it was in a low, measured voice. "I do not like the idea that you involved a civilian in this investigation."

"But…"

"No 'buts.'" Gressley's voice lowered to almost a whisper. "You've done a good job so far, so I'm going to keep you on the case. But you better not pull another crazy stunt like this. I don't want our investigation to resemble the Keystone Cops. Also, I don't want you seeing Mr. Bill Boyd again until this case is over. Do you understand?"

"Clearly, sir."

Gressley relaxed. "You did a good job following up on what happened last night, so don't be too upset with yourself. But the next time something happens like this, make sure you call me."

Toby asked, "What if you're not home?"

Gressley hesitated, remembering what he was doing at the time Toby was at the Hotel Marion. A slight smile crossed his face. "Then call Sylvia; she'll know where to find me. I liked your idea about a bigger car. I called Chief Chambers last night, and he agreed. Petit's Motors will be sending over a touring car this morning."

Toby nodded.

Gressley said, "I have to meet with the chief. You stay here until we are ready to start today's investigation." Gressley stood up and walked out of the room. If Toby had not been so preoccupied with his feelings, he might have noticed Gressley stop at Sylvia's desk for a brief conversation before he went into Chief Chambers' office. However, Toby did notice a salesman from Petit's standing at Sylvia's desk a few minutes later.

After the salesman left, Sylvia made three phone calls. One was to the Hotel Marion to verify that Mr. Reynolds would be in meetings until four o'clock in the afternoon, with an hour break for lunch. The second was to Lieutenant Leffets of the Lansing police, to see if he would be available for an important phone call from Detective Gressley.

The third call was much longer and more delicate. When Sylvia was done, she walked into Gressley's office where Toby was still sitting. She placed an envelope on Gressley's desk. Then she turned to Toby and said, "Come on, we have some work to do."

"But Gressley told me to stay here."

Sylvia smiled. "He just gave me instructions for you to come with me to interview Port Huron's leading madam—Velvet Cushion."

Toby and Sylvia got into the touring car. Toby said, "You got to be kidding! She's going to be at your house?"

"It's important that we talk to her. She obviously wouldn't come to the station and didn't want us going to her place of business. So we agreed that my house would be a suitable location."

"I still can't believe we're going to be interviewing Velvet Cushion."

Sylvia giggled. "Well, believe it buster. And don't make any cracks about her name."

Toby asked, "Why is it we allow houses of prostitution in the First Ward?"

"I think it's a matter of priorities. The city has other crimes that are considered more serious."

"But our minister thinks it's a shame we allow this immoral behavior to exist only a couple of blocks from the main business district."

"At least the police monitor the houses. And they do raid them if the owners are committing other crimes. Velvet's establishment has enjoyed a fine reputation for ten years. Also, she's maintained what you might call good relations with a couple of the city officials."

Toby groaned.

Sylvia smiled. "Do you know anything about Velvet?"

"No."

"She's a surprisingly sophisticated woman. But she can be very tough. I doubt if she could be successful in that business without being made of iron."

Despite Sylvia's description, Toby was totally surprised by the appearance of Velvet Cushion. She was in her midfifties, short, slim, and dressed to the nines. She exhibited considerable poise, and her voice sounded like she was a product of an expensive finishing school.

The three sat around Sylvia's kitchen table. "Thank you for seeing us, Velvet, er, ah, Miss Cushion." Toby felt a sudden urge to laugh. Enough of a grin must have been apparent, because Sylvia instantly delivered a sharp kick to his shin.

"Please call me Velvet. I understand you are interested in knowing about a girl called Charla. Her real name is Charlotte Clemon. She started working for me about three years ago when she moved here from Lansing. She was one of my most talented girls, very attractive. Girls of her caliber often have relations with very rich, influential men who do not want to be seen at my house. They demand utmost discretion."

"Did she get into any difficulties?"

"She was very successful at first. But after about eighteen months, I became dissatisfied with her performance."

Her 'performance' indeed! Toby thought. He asked, "In what way?" He glanced quickly at Sylvia, who sat with her foot pointed in his direction.

"Clients began to complain that she wanted more of a relationship than just the occasional evening. I warned her a couple times that her behavior was inappropriate, but she ignored me. So I had no alternative but to fire her. The last I heard, she was in Detroit."

"Do you have any idea where she might stay, if she was in town?" Toby asked.

"Sometimes she would stay at a boardinghouse a few blocks from here." Velvet wrote down the address. "If there are no more questions, Patrolman Sharpe, I need to go back to work."

Standing, Toby said, "Thank you for helping us out."

Velvet touched Toby's belt lightly with the tip of her parasol. "If you ever want to visit my establishment, please do. Just don't wear your uniform."

Toby's face flamed red. "I won't. I mean…"

Velvet smiled mischievously. As she turned to leave, she said, "And I do like your new zipper."

CHAPTER 17

▼

Gressley left his meeting with Chief Chambers and returned to his desk. He sat down and sighed in relief. He had not been sure if the chief would allow Sylvia to continue helping with the investigation. But when Gressley explained how helpful she had been so far and assured him that Sylvia would not be placed in harm's way, Chief Chambers said it would be OK. He knew that Sylvia would be pleased. Ever since Alice Wells became the first policewoman in America when she was hired by the Los Angeles police department in 1910, Sylvia had been pushing for a similar appointment.

Gressley opened the envelope Sylvia had placed on his desk and laughed. It contained a newspaper photograph of Alice Wells and three other policewomen working in Los Angeles. She had scrawled across the photo, "Los Angeles 4, Port Huron 0." He placed the photo in his desk and went to the telephone to make a long distance call.

"Lansing police."

"Good morning, may I talk to Lieutenant Leffets? This is Detective John Gressley from the Port Huron police."

"Yes, detective. He told me that you would be calling."

Hugh Leffets was Gressley's best friend when he worked for the Lansing police department. They had maintained sporadic contact since he moved to Port Huron.

"Hi, John. How are you doing?"

"Hello, Hugh. Things are fine. How are you and your family?"

"Things are going well. Alice is planning to get married in September."

"Your daughter is old enough to get married? I don't believe it."

Hugh asked, "How about you? Are you seeing anyone?"

Gressley hesitated for a moment. He was reluctant to tell Hugh about Sylvia. He knew how quickly information was passed from one police department to another. He said, "No one special right now."

"That's too bad. We're sending you an invitation to Alice's wedding. I hope you're able to come."

"I'll be there."

Hugh said, "Good. Now what's your urgent call about?"

"I have some questions about a state employee named Edgar Reynolds."

Hugh said, "I got a lot of questions about that guy."

"How so?"

"I think his case came up two or three years after you left. We had complaints from parents about him taking naked pictures of their kids. Seems he has a knack for finding fourteen- and fifteen-year-olds who are rebellious and want to do something adventurous. He would get them to pose, saying that no one would ever find out."

Gressley asked, "Why wasn't he arrested?"

"When push came to shove, none of the families were willing to press charges. We did manage to put enough pressure on him that he stopped taking pictures. We think he has a photo collection of about twenty different kids—boys and girls."

"Couldn't the prosecutor do anything without the cooperation of the families?"

Hugh said, "According to the prosecutor, there just wasn't enough evidence to bring a case. As I understand it, our pornography laws are based on an English ruling of 1868 that relates only to public acts of pornography. Since Reynolds never has made these public, it's unclear what the charge would be."

"Did he ever molest any of the children?"

"Not as far as we know. He was just interested in taking pictures. Apparently, he regards it as some kind of art form."

Gressley asked, "Do you remember any families in particular?"

"Yeah. The most bizarre case was with the Clemon family."

"Wait a minute. You said the last name was Clemon?"

Hugh said, "Yes. Why?"

"We're looking for a young woman with a last name that sounds like that. Her first name is Charlotte."

"That was this girl's first name. She came to talk to me. She was really upset about the pictures. But about a week later her father shows up. He tells us that it was just a wild story his daughter made up to get some attention. Remembering how upset the girl was, we knew her father's story was bull. But we couldn't do anything about it."

"What happened after that?"

Hugh said, "Charlotte got really wild. She got into drugs and prostitution and then moved away. I don't know where she is now. Her mother committed suicide about five years ago. But here's the sickest thing: her father and Reynolds are still friends. Who knows, maybe Reynolds shares other photos with him. Why do you want to know about Reynolds anyway?"

"He's in Port Huron right now. He's part of a murder investigation."

"Dexter Conroy? I read about that in today's paper."

Gressley said, "Right. Reynolds is in town talking to county officials about the feasibility of building cement roads. He was seen talking to Conroy on the *Tashmoo* Saturday. They were arguing about something. Then last night some lady of the night stole an envelope from his room. It could possibly be Charlotte Clemon."

"Sounds like you got a couple of rats in your lovely town. Conroy couldn't be trusted any farther than you could throw him. And as big as he was, that wouldn't have been far."

"I wonder if this has anything to do with the roads that are being planned. What's your opinion of Reynolds as a government official?"

Hugh said, "He's pretty honest, as far as I know. But there is a lot of money that's going to go into paving roads. Much of it will go into somebody's greedy pocket if we're not careful."

"I don't suppose Conroy would be above a little blackmail. What do you think?"

"Ha. I wouldn't be surprised at all. Tell you what John. I'll make a point of being here all day. If you need any help putting that creep Reynolds in jail, be sure to call."

Gressley said, "You can count on it. Thanks for the information. Congratulate Alice for me."

*   *   *   *

The desk sergeant knocked on Detective Cedric Alexander's door. Alexander motioned him in. "What is it?"

"A constable on the west side of town wants to talk to you. He thinks he might have some information on the missing girls you're looking for. He's on the phone."

Alexander walked into the main office area. "It certainly will be nice when we have phones in our private offices."

The sergeant laughed. "I'm sure we'll all be retired before that happens."

Detective Alexander picked up the receiver and spoke into the wall phone's mouthpiece. "Alexander here."

"Morning, sir. I don't know if this is worth anything or not, but I thought I'd call anyway."

"What happened?"

"A man came to the police station this morning, complaining about a ruckus he heard last night. We went to the house where he said he heard screams. It was an abandoned house, but the man said he had seen a couple of men going in and out of it the past couple of days."

Alexander asked, "What's the address?"

"1842 Wicker Street."

"Did you go to the house?"

"Yes, sir. We found evidence that a horse had been kept in a shed. When we went inside the house, we found some dirty women's clothes and rotten food that had been thrown in a trash can. We also found boxes from a department store. There was a receipt in one of the boxes showing that blouses, skirts, and under-garments had been purchased yesterday."

Alexander asked, "Can you tell how many people might have been there?"

"Judging from the food and plates, I would guess four."

"Good work, constable. Go back to the house; I will be there in fifteen minutes."

Alexander replaced the receiver and walked quickly to the sergeant at the front desk. "I want you to contact all the police stations in cities that border on Lake Ontario, Lake Erie, and Lake Huron, and tell them to be on the lookout for two young women who have been kidnapped and are being taken to the United States to be sold into white slavery. There are probably two men with them."

"That's a lot of cities."

"I know, but we have to do it. Start with Kingston and work your way to Sarnia."

"That will take several hours to complete."

Alexander grabbed his hat and rushed for the door. He shouted, "Then you'd better start right now!"

*   *   *   *

Toby parked in front of the boardinghouse. Sylvia began to get out of the car. Toby touched her arm, and said, "Sorry Sylvia, but I better do this myself. I'm in enough trouble already over what happened last night."

"But this is different. Bill did something illegal. Besides, I was the one who got you the interview with Velvet."

"Yes, but you're not a policeman."

Sylvia's eyes flashed with anger. "You don't need to tell me."

Toby took a few steps, feeling Sylvia's eyes boring into the back of his head. Then he thought about how flustered he was when Velvet poked her parasol at him. He also remembered the story about how Gressley got into trouble in a similar situation in Lansing. He turned around and said, "Maybe it wouldn't be such a bad idea if you came along. From what Velvet said, Charla can be pretty manipulative. It might be better if a woman is in the room when I talk to her."

"Now that's what I call sound judgment!" Sylvia said as she bounded from the car.

Sitting on the porch, the owner of the boardinghouse watched the two figures get out of the car. She thought, *What's this? Looks like a kid cop who doesn't look very sure of himself and a middle-aged woman with enough confidence for the two of them.*

The pair turned onto Mrs. Jenkins' sidewalk and approached her house. *Jee-sus, Mary, and Joseph. Why are they coming here?*

Toby said, "Good morning, Mrs. Jenkins. I'm Patrolman Sharpe and this is Sylvia Pointe."

"You mean like a lead pencil? You know—a sharp point."

Toby smiled politely while Sylvia rolled her eyes. They had heard this joke about a dozen times in the office and never thought it was funny. Toby said, "We're looking for a young woman who goes by the name of Charla. Is she staying here?"

"She's in room five. But she doesn't do any hanky-panky here. All she does is come here to sleep."

"I'm sure that's true. But it's important we talk to her."

"Be my guest."

Toby knocked on the door to room five. Charla opened the door.

"Charla?"

"Yes."

"We're from the Port Huron police department. May we come in and ask you a few questions?"

Charla took a careful look at Toby as she backed away from the doorway to allow them to enter. She asked, "Do I know you?"

"I don't know."

"Yeah, you were at the Hotel Marion last night."

"If you don't mind," said Sylvia, "we're here to ask the questions."

Toby said, "For one, is your real name Charlotte Clemon?"

"Yes."

Toby asked, "Were you originally from Lansing?"

"Yes."

"Were you acquainted with Dexter Conroy when you worked for Velvet Cushion?"

"Is that the man who got killed?" Charla asked.

"That's right."

Charla sat down on the bed. "I think I might have been with him a few times."

"We've been told that someone matching your description was going to marry Mr. Conroy after he got a divorce."

"If you know everything about me, why are you asking all these questions?"

Toby said, "We're trying to collect as much accurate information as possible."

Charla stared at the floor.

Toby asked, "So how well did you know Mr. Conroy? Before you answer, you should know that we have already talked to his secretary."

"All right. We were going to be married, but he called it off a couple of weeks ago."

"Why?"

Charla screamed, "I don't know! Stop asking me these questions."

Toby said, "I just have a few more. Where were you Saturday night?"

"I was in Detroit. I didn't get into Port Huron until Sunday morning."

"Do you have anyone who can verify that?"

Charla kneaded the bedspread with her right hand. "No. I was alone Saturday night."

"Do you know a man by the name Edgar Reynolds?"

Charla felt her body tense. She guessed that there might be a connection between the patrolman and the man she hit in Reynolds' room. *But I can't tell them about Reynolds*, she thought. *I just can't.* Breathing deeply, she willed herself to remain calm. "I've heard the name, but I don't think I've ever met him."

Sylvia spotted an envelope on the dresser. She asked, "What was in here?"

Charla replied, "Oh, just some letters. I threw them away."

Sylvia asked, "Do you mind if we take it with us? We'll have you sign for it and will return it if you want."

Charla hesitated. Then she said, "Sure, take it. I don't want it anymore."

Toby and Sylvia left the room and returned to the car.

Sylvia waved the envelope in Toby's face. She said, "I think we have some strong evidence here."

"Why?"

"Look at this tear in the corner. It was caused by something other than just opening it. I bet it will match the paper you got from Reynolds' room."

Toby said, "Holy smokes! I think you're right."

Sylvia said, "I think you should stay here to watch the house while I have this checked out."

"You're going to walk back?"

"Of course not. I'm going to drive."

"But you don't know how to drive!"

"How hard can it be? I watched you, and I think I understand how it's done. So if you would just start this tin Lizzie for me, I'll be on my way."

"All right. But send someone over here to take my place. I don't want to stand around here all day. And don't forget to have the envelope fingerprinted."

Sylvia got behind the wheel. "I'll send someone as soon as I get back to the station."

Toby cringed in anticipation.

Sylvia actually got off to a smooth start, except she was going backward. She stopped the car.

Toby said, "You might want to try first gear, not reverse."

She smiled as she shifted into first. The car shot ahead and began to whine as it accelerated.

Toby thought, *Maybe I'll tell her about second gear tomorrow.*

Toby positioned himself where he could see the front door of the boarding-house as well as Charla's window. Nearly dozing off, he was suddenly jerked awake by an intriguing thought. If road construction is tied in with the murder, maybe Bill Boyd's knowledge about that subject could help.

Toby looked up to see Patrolman Wilbur Greene approaching on a bicycle. Greene got off the bike. He asked, "So what's so important?"

Toby said, "One of the murder suspects is in that boardinghouse."

"You mean the boardinghouse owned by those mackerel-snappers?"

"Who?"

Greene smirked. "Catholics. Too many of them movin' to Port Huron if you ask me."

"The woman we are watching is named Charla."

"Charla? The one from Velvet's?"

Toby said, "You know her?"

Greene laughed, "You might say that I *know* her."

"You've had sexual intercourse with her?"

"Not exactly."

Toby thought, *jeez, how do you not exactly have intercourse?* He asked, "What do you mean, 'not exactly?'"

"She's too expensive for me. But I've seen her at Velvet's a couple of times."

"Good, you know what she looks like. I want you to keep an eye on the boardinghouse, and call the station if she leaves."

"How am I going to do that?"

"Mrs. Jenkins has a phone. You can use it." Toby grabbed the bike and peddled furiously back to the police station.

*   *   *   *

Charla saw Toby take off on the bicycle. She thought, *I've got to get out of here!*

Mrs. Jenkins rapped sharply on Charla's door. "Young lady, I want you gone as soon as possible. Your reputation is bad enough, but I won't have the police standing out on the street looking at my house."

"I agree. Could I use your phone to call someone to help me move?"

"Yes, but be quick about it."

The two women walked into Mrs. Jenkins' apartment. Charla rang the operator, and gave the number she wanted. Turning to Mrs. Jenkins, she asked, "Do you mind if I have some privacy?"

Mrs. Jenkins stared at Charla for a moment and then retreated. Pausing briefly at the door, she heard Charla say, "Dex, can you come and get me? I really need your help."

Dexter asked, "What's wrong?"

Charla made sure Mrs. Jenkins was out of the room before she answered. "The police just came here asking questions about your dad. I think it would be good if I got out of town."

"Did you say you knew him?"

Charla said, "Yes. I told them that we were going to get married. I couldn't help it because they had already talked to that nosy secretary of your dad's. Can you help me?"

"Yeah, what do you want?"

"Bring me some men's clothing. I want to get out of here without the police knowing."

Dexter asked, "Shoes and everything?"

"Yes. Can you be here in thirty minutes?"

"Thirty minutes? Sure."

▼

CHAPTER 18

Narrowly missing a couple pedestrians, Toby wondered what he was going to say to Gressley. *How about, I know I'm not supposed to see Bill until this case is over, but maybe I could just talk to him. I think he might be able to help us.* Skidding to a stop in front of the City Hall, he dropped the bike and ran to the door. Noticing the rented touring car parked about four feet from the curb, he thanked God Sylvia made it back to the police station and hoped she didn't kill anyone.

As he reached Gressley's door, he said, "Detective, I have..." He was unable to complete the sentence because his jaw dropped. Gressley's desk was blanketed with a map of Michigan. Seated across from the detective were Sylvia Sharpe and Bill Boyd!

Gressley said, "Ah, Tobias. I'm glad you got back so soon. I remembered a conversation we had about cars and roads yesterday. It occurred to me that Mr. Boyd might redeem himself for last night by giving us a lecture on those subjects. He's just about to start. Close the door and take a seat."

Although Bill looked like he was suffering from a hangover, he wasn't going to forfeit this opportunity to put on a show. Sounding like a ringmaster at a Barnum & Bailey circus, he began his presentation. "Toby, please bring your chair close to the desk so I can provide you and your partners in crime fighting with information that will dazzle your mind." Sylvia grinned, Gressley appeared stoic, and Toby thought, *jeez Bill, can't you play it straight just once?*

Now that Toby was seated, Bill drew a circle around the counties of St. Clair, Tuscola, Huron, Sanilac, and Lapeer. "As you all know, this is the area commonly known as Michigan's Thumb. Two interurban lines end at Imlay City and

Port Huron. If you live close to those lines, you have fairly easy access to the Detroit area.

"But most of the rural population is too far away from the interurban for it to be of much use. If these people want to travel, they must do it on gravel or dirt roads. These are OK for the horse and buggy but will not hold up to the rigors of automobiles.

"States are becoming aware of the fact that people want cars. They also know the only roads that will accommodate steady automobile use are concrete ones. Outside of the cities, there are fewer than 500 miles of concrete roads in the United States. But since Henry Ford is now selling cars for less than $600, more and more people can buy them. Residents in rural areas who have little access to public transportation are really going to want them.

"So, my dear friends, I predict that in the next few years there will be a building frenzy. States and counties are now forming road commissions who will be supervising the construction of highways made of concrete. When that happens it will not be long, my dear enforcers of the law, until the popularity of the automobile will make the interurban obsolete."

Gressley cringed at that observation.

Sylvia asked, "Why don't they extend the interurban line? It seems like that would be cheaper."

"Cheaper to construct, perhaps," answered Bill. "But there would not be enough customers in the rural areas to make it profitable for a private company. Plus, I believe more and more Americans want the independence of owing their own motor car."

Boyd drew a line down the middle of Michigan's Thumb connecting Port Austin, Bad Axe, Marlette, and Imlay City. He said, "Now, look at this route through the Thumb. This is but one example of towns that will someday be linked by these ribbons of concrete. If you start connecting other cities, it will mean hundreds of miles of roads just in the Thumb. And, of course, this will generate big bucks for the contractors who provide the material. And lots of money always attracts the greedy."

Toby asked, "When do you think this road construction will take place?"

"For St. Clair County, it will be this year. Consider how quickly things are moving. The voters approved the establishment of the St. Clair County Road Commission in April. It met for the first time earlier this month, when it elected Charles Bailey as its chairman."

Boyd made a small mark on the map about one mile north of Marine City. "The road commission has already agreed to unleash a road roller, a scarifier, and swarms of laborers in this area to build the first concrete road in the county outside of the city limits of Port Huron.

"It also proposed three trunk line roads that will eventually become state roads, as well as four county roads." Boyd pointed at the map again. "Let me show you one example. If approved, trunk line number one will start at Port Huron and go south through Marysville and St. Clair to Marine City. Then it will head west to Anchorville."

Gressley said, "You've been very helpful, Bill. We appreciate you taking time to see us today."

Bill tossed his pencil on the table. "You're welcome. Now it's my turn to ask a question. What is the Port Huron police department doing about white slavery?"

Gressley frowned. "What exactly do you mean?"

"Are you doing anything to help the women who are kidnapped in Canada and smuggled into Port Huron?"

"Do you have any specific information about his type of activity?"

Bill paused. "No. But several credible people have given convincing arguments that it happens."

Gressley said, "I feel sorry for any woman who is victimized in that way, but I have no concrete information to act on. We can't just sit someone in a boat on the St. Clair River and expect to find a kidnapper. Our limited staff has enough to do solving crimes we know about."

Bill stood up. "I know—it's always about money. But something has to be done for those women."

Sylvia walked Bill to the door. "How's your head?"

"It feels better now than when I got up this morning. I went to my doctor earlier today, and he didn't think there was anything to worry about. He said to take some aspirin and rest for a few days. So I think I'm going to go home now and rest for a while."

"Well, take care of yourself. We really do appreciate you coming in today."

Gressley watched Sylvia as she returned to his office. He said, "That's quite a flamboyant friend you have, Tobias."

"He's been like that ever since I have known him. It's gotten him in trouble a few times, but I couldn't ask for a better chum."

Sylvia returned to the office and sat down.

Gressley said, "Let's share any new information we gathered this morning. I found out that Charla's real name is Charlotte Clemon, and she's from Lansing. Reynolds took nude photographs of her when she was about fifteen. When Charla's father found out about the pictures, he kicked her out of the house."

Sylvia said, "That's terrible. I hope Reynolds was punished."

"He wasn't. He was able to keep everything private."

Sylvia slammed her notebook on the table.

"That would certainly give Charla a motive to steal the envelope from Reynolds if it contained the pictures," Toby said. "But why kill Conroy?"

Sylvia said, "What if Conroy had the photos and gave them back to Reynolds when they got to Port Huron? Charla might have killed Conroy if she thought he still had them."

Gressley nodded. "Or Reynolds might have murdered Conroy to get them back. Remember, they got into an argument on the *Tashmoo*. Maybe Conroy was blackmailing Reynolds. After all, Reynolds would be embarrassed and perhaps taken to court if the pictures were made public. And I'm sure he would lose his job."

Toby asked, "But how would Conroy find out about the photographs?"

Sylvia said, "Maybe Reynolds showed them to him."

Toby asked, "Did we find out anything about the envelope we took from Charla's room?"

Sylvia opened a folder. "See how the piece of paper Toby brought back from the hotel matches the tear in the envelope we got from Charla? I think we can safely say that she's the thief."

Toby said, "She and Reynolds look like good murder suspects too."

"Yes, but we shouldn't forget about Mrs. Conroy and the son," Gressley said. "They both had much to gain from Conroy's death."

Their discussion was interrupted with a knock on the door.

Gressley said, "Come in."

Sergeant Williams entered the office. "We just caught a kid breaking into a house. I think he's the person who broke into the hotels."

"What happened?"

"He broke into a house occupied by a family that recently came here from Scotland. He thought the house was empty. The kitchen window was open, so he cut the screen and crawled in." The Sergeant's chin began to quiver as he tried not to laugh.

Gressley noted Williams' odd behavior. He said, "Just take a minute to relax Sergeant. What did he do to the family?"

Williams gave a lopsided grin. "Uh, no sir. He didn't do anything to them. It seems that just about the time he got to the living room, someone started playing the bagpipes. He screamed and wet his pants. The family wrestled him to the floor. A feisty ten-year-old girl sat on his back, while her father and older brother tied his hands and feet."

Toby laughed, "It doesn't sound like the poor kid had a chance."

Williams nodded, "That's right. According to the Scottish father they held him 'doon so he couldnae get oot of the hoose.'"

The room erupted in laughter. After a few moments, Gressley asked, "What's the boy's name?"

"Luke Laboy."

Gressley asked, "Toby, what were the marks carved into the chair in Reynolds' room?"

"It was either seventy-seven or LL. Do you think he's the one who broke into the hotels and left his initials?"

Williams said, "Yep. His fingerprints matched the ones Toby got from the hotels. When I told him that his fingerprints were found in the hotel rooms, he said he was paid to do it by a woman named Charla."

"Good work, Sergeant."

Gressley turned to Toby. "Get back to the boardinghouse and arrest Charla. I'm going to walk over to the Marion and confront Mr. Reynolds."

"What am I going to charge her with?" Toby asked.

"For now, charge her with breaking and entering. We'll consider a murder charge later."

*   *   *   *

Mary Sharpe sat in the living room playing with her daughter. She wore a dark blue skirt and a white blouse. The skirt was the latest style, nearly two inches above the ankle, with four-inch slits on both sides. When a familiar figure appeared on the porch Amanda pointed her finger and yelled, "Gramma!"

Ruth Sharpe opened the screen door and entered the house. "Hello, everyone!"

Mary stood up. "Hi, mother. It's so nice of you to take care of Chris and Amanda today."

"Oh, say nothing of it, Mary. I love spending time with my grandchildren." Ruth Sharpe looked at Mary's skirt. "Are you going to wear that skirt in public?"

Mary frowned. "What's wrong with it?"

"It's so short. And those slits on the sides expose your legs."

"Most young women are wearing their skirts this way. It makes getting in and out of cars and trolleys much easier."

Ruth gave another disapproving look at Mary's skirt. "What exactly are your meetings about today?"

"Did you hear about the speaker who was at the Ladies Library Association Saturday?"

"No. What was her speech about?"

"Myra Cullenbine, a woman from Chicago, spoke about white slave trade," Mary said.

"White slave trade? What's that?"

"It's when women are abducted and forced to work in factories, sold as wives, or forced to become prostitutes."

Ruth said, "Upon my soul, that's a terrible thing to listen to!"

"I think it's a terrible thing that is happening to young women. And some people think hundreds of them are being smuggled into Port Huron each year."

Ruth clutched her throat. "It's unbelievable that those things could happen in our community."

"Unfortunately, I believe it's true. We're meeting with representatives from the Life-Saving Service and the Customs Service to see if there's anything they can do to help."

"Who's 'we'?"

Mary said, "Donna, Leah, and Nancy are going with me."

"What good is it for women to trouble their minds over these things? That's business best left to men. We have enough to do taking care of our families."

"The success Jane Addams had with her Hull House project in Chicago is a good example of how women can accomplish just as much as men."

"Fiddlesticks," Ruth said. "Jane Addams has sacrificed her femininity. Why, she actually brags that she's never worn a corset."

Mary picked up her purse and parasol. "Maybe we can continue this discussion later. I need to leave now or I'll miss the trolley. Thanks again for watching Chris and Amanda." She kissed her children and hurried out the door.

Ruth Sharpe watched her daughter-in-law walk down the street. She muttered, "Stuff and nonsense. This younger generation is a bunch of troublemakers if you ask me."

*   *   *   *

Detective Gressley was about to leave the police station for his confrontation with Edgar Reynolds when Sylvia called him over to her desk. She was holding the envelope taken from Charla's room.

She said, "I have an idea."

"What?"

She picked up a blank sheet of paper. "What do you think of putting this paper in the envelope? Then when you meet with Reynolds, you tell him you want him to come back to the police station so you can see if his fingerprints match those on the envelope as well as its contents. We'll keep the envelope here so he won't have any idea what is in it when you see him at the hotel."

"But we haven't had time to take the envelope to Smith's Photography."

Sylvia smiled, "Reynolds doesn't know that."

"That's a really good idea. Whatever was in that envelope, he probably didn't want anybody to know he had it. If he thinks we have the contents, he might panic. On the other hand, if he's willing to come back to the station, I didn't lie to him about what was in the envelope. Sylvia, you would make a darn good policeman."

"Thanks, but make that 'policewoman.'"

Gressley smiled as he put on his hat and walked out of the office. He said, "Go ahead and put the paper in the envelope. I'm ready to pay a visit on Reynolds."

*   *   *   *

Edgar Reynolds had just finished his morning session and was walking to the hotel's dining room when Gressley addressed him. "Mr. Reynolds? I'm Detective John Gressley of the Port Huron Police. May I have a few minutes of your time?"

Reynolds frowned. "Does this have anything to with what happened in my room last night?"

"Yes."

"Good, but it will have to be short. I'm having lunch with Charles Bailey, chairman of the St. Clair County Road Commission and other political officials."

Gressley said, "I'm sorry, but this is going to intrude on your plans. We have an envelope that I believe was stolen from your room. In order to confirm that belief, I want you to come with me to the police station so we can take your fingerprints. Then we can compare your prints with the ones on the envelope as well as its contents."

Reynolds' eyes widened in panic. "What do you mean?"

"I think you know what I mean. Or do I have to call Lieutenant Leffets of the Lansing police?"

Reynolds' face flushed scarlet. "I can't go right now."

Gressley's gray eyes narrowed as he took a step closer to Reynolds. "I believe it is in your best interest to come with me. As a state official, I don't think you want to be seen being arrested in a hotel lobby."

Reynolds' Adam's apple began to bob. He managed a shrill squeak. "OK. Let's get this over with."

When they approached the hotel door, Reynolds suddenly shoved Gressley into a table, sending the detective sprawling onto the floor. Gressley's shoulder hit a spittoon, spilling its putrid contents.

Reynolds ran frantically out the door, where he nearly collided with a horse-drawn delivery wagon. He pulled the surprised driver off the seat and threw him onto the street. Reynolds jumped on the wagon and hit the horse sharply with the reins. The horse, shocked by the painful slap to its backside, galloped down Huron Avenue toward the Black River.

Gressley quickly recovered. He commandeered a bicycle and took off after Reynolds. The terrorized horse thundered down the street, widening the gap between itself and the pursuer on the bicycle. However, as Reynolds approached the Black River, the bridge master yelled that the bridge was going up.

When Reynolds reached the bridge, it had begun its ascent. He clamored down from the wagon and ran up the drawbridge, hoping that if he was fast enough, he could jump to the other side. He soon realized the futility of his attempt because the distance between the two halves of the bridge was too great for a successful jump.

The angle of the bridge was now so steep that Reynolds found himself sliding backward. Frantically, he grasped the side railing. Gressley dismounted from his bicycle and watched Reynolds as he hung helplessly onto the side railing, his legs flailing.

The bridge master began to lower the bridge. Then he suddenly stopped, causing the bridge to quiver. Reynolds lost his grip and tumbled to the street. He screamed, "I hurt my knee!"

Gressley picked him up. "Mr. Reynolds, you're under arrest for the murder of Dexter Conroy."

"What? I didn't kill anyone! I thought you were going to arrest me because of my art."

"We can discuss the legality of your so-called art later. For now, I want to know why you should not be arrested for murder." He handcuffed Reynolds and began walking him toward the police station.

The angry horse bared his teeth and snorted at the two men as they passed by.

CHAPTER 19

▼

Mrs. Jenkins answered the knock at her boardinghouse door and looked suspiciously at the young man holding a paper bag full of clothes.

Dexter Conway said, "I'm here to see Charla."

Peering at the policeman standing on the corner, Mrs. Jenkins opened the door. "Fine, go right to her room—number five."

Dexter knocked on Charla's door.

Charla opened the door. She said, "Oh, Dex! You are a friend."

Dexter looked at Charla in amazement. Her hair was cut short, all makeup was removed from her face, and her nails were trimmed. "You sure look a lot different."

She handed him a section of a torn bedsheet. "I'm going to look even less like myself after you tie this around my chest. Did you bring everything I asked for?"

Dexter tied the ends of the bedsheet. "I think so. Check and see."

Charla quickly changed into one of Dexter's old suits. "How do I look?"

"Fine, except the pants are a little baggy."

"Well, it's got to do." She went to the door. "Mrs. Jenkins, could you come in for a minute. I want to settle up."

Mrs. Jenkins laughed as she entered the room. "Halloween's a little early ain't it?"

Charla never bothered to answer as Dexter wrapped his left arm around Mrs. Jenkins' ample waist and clamped his right hand on her mouth. He then shoved her onto a chair.

Charla quickly bound her feet and wrists to the chair and gagged her mouth. "Sorry we've got to do this, but I can't risk you calling the cops as soon as we leave."

Charla threw several dollar bills on the floor. "This should cover my bill."

Charla walked to Mrs. Jenkins's room and called the railroad station. "When is the next train leaving Port Huron?"

"That would be the 12:45 to Flint, Lansing, and Chicago."

Charla hung up. "Can you take me to the railroad station?"

"Sure."

Charla started to leave the house. Dexter grabbed her arm. "Wait a minute. You can't walk like that."

"What do you mean?"

"You're hips are swinging too much. People will think something's weird."

"How can I do it differently?"

"Try walking with your toes pointed in."

Dexter watched Charla take a few steps. "That's better."

Charla said, "When we leave the boardinghouse, walk between me and that cop on the corner. That way he won't get a good look at me."

Minutes later patrolman Greene saw what he believed to be two men leave the boardinghouse and get into a shiny yellow Pierce-Arrow.

*   *   *   *

Toby arrived at the boardinghouse minutes after Charla and Dexter departed. Toby looked across the street at Patrolman Wilbur Greene, who was in a catcher's crouch, banging his nightstick on the sidewalk.

When Greene saw Toby getting out of the car, he stood up and wiped off his nightstick. He said, "I've been killing ants. I'm up to forty-two."

That's funny, Toby thought. *I'm trying to catch a killer and Wilbur's squatting there hammering ants.* Toby walked across the street. He asked, "Anything going on in the boardinghouse?"

"Not much. Just a couple of men who left in a Pierce-Arrow a couple of minutes ago."

"Pierce-Arrow? Was it yellow?"

Wilbur said, "Yeah."

"What did they look like?"

"The man who drove the Pierce-Arrow was built like you, only a little flabbier. The other person was about the same height but thinner. And his pants were baggy in the seat."

Toby said, "The driver might have been Dexter Conroy. Are you sure the second person was a man?"

"Don't you think I can tell the difference between a man and a woman?"

"Depends how good the disguise was. And maybe you were concentrating too much on killing ants to get a good look."

Wilbur glared at Toby. "Doing your job is boring."

They walked to the boardinghouse and knocked on the door. Nobody answered, but Wilbur thought he heard something inside. They entered the house. The sound became louder as they hurried down the hallway to Charla's room. They opened the door to see that Mrs. Jenkins had managed to tip the chair over. She was lying on her back, with her dress nearly over her head, as she kicked the wall with her feet. Toby removed the gag from her mouth.

She gasped, "What are you two starin' at? Pull my dress down and untie me!"

As Toby was untying her, he asked her what happened.

Mrs. Jenkins said, "Charla and her boyfriend jumped me and tied me up so I couldn't call the police."

Wilbur asked, "Do you know where they were headed?"

"The train station. I heard Charla say they were going to catch the 12:45 to Chicago."

The patrolmen ran to the car, jumped in, and headed downtown. After they had driven for a few minutes, Toby said, "I wish we had taken time to call the railroad station and asked them to hold the train."

"It's too late now. Can't you make this thing go any faster?"

"No. It's too bad we don't have a telephone in the car."

Wilbur laughed. "That's stupid. Where would you put all the wires?"

Toby shrugged. "It was just an idea."

Wilbur said crossly, "I have an idea. Why is Sylvia working on the murder case, instead of a policeman like me?"

A *policeman like you would be the last person I would want to be working with,* Toby thought. He said, "She's not really doing police work. All she's done so far is to make a couple of telephone calls for Gressley and arrange a meeting with Velvet Cushion."

"I know how I would have 'arranged a meeting.' I would have knocked down Velvet's door and made her talk. I think Sylvia ought to stay home where women belong. And what's that big shot Gressley think he's doing?"

Toby remembered the conversation he overheard in the restroom yesterday. Toby asked, "You mean that Gressley's a know-it-all don't you? And I'm his errand boy?"

Wilbur's eyes narrowed. "Sergeant Williams has a big mouth."

Toby gripped the steering wheel tightly. "He didn't tell me. But do you know what's interesting? All the time we've been in this car, you haven't asked me anything about the case. All you've done is criticize people. Maybe you ought to be quiet unless you want to talk about the murder investigation."

Wilbur stared at Toby but didn't say anything. Both men remained silent until they approached downtown. In front of them was a line of cars, horses, and bicycles waiting to cross the Black River. Wilbur said, "It looks like the draw-bridge is up."

Toby nodded. "Let's hope the Pierce-Arrow is still on this side of the river."

*　　*　　*　　*

Dexter and Charla had been stopped by the Military Street drawbridge and were waiting impatiently for it to be lowered. Charla glanced to the right and saw Edgar Reynolds in handcuffs, being marched down the street. She pulled the hat down over her face, hoping she would not be recognized.

When the bridge was lowered, traffic began to move. Minutes later, Dexter pulled into the railroad station parking lot in the south end of town. The two passengers got out and walked quickly to the station's entrance.

As they approached the door, Dexter spoke. "Charla, this may not be the best time to talk about this, but I'd do anything for you. Would you give me another chance?"

"I'm sorry Dex, but I don't think that's possible."

"Why not? We had a good thing going last year."

"That's the point. Once you passed me over to your dad, we could never be anything other than friends."

"I didn't 'pass you over.' He took you. He said that if I wouldn't let him have you, he'd cut me off without a dime."

"I just can't spend my life with someone who doesn't have enough guts to stand up to his father. If you were a man…"

Dexter's temper flared. "I'll show you who's a man." He slapped her hard in the face.

Wiping blood from the corner of her mouth, Charla glared at Dexter. "You're a man all right, just like your dad. Forget what I said about a friendship. Good-bye." She turned to enter the railroad station.

"Oh God, I'm sorry. I'll never do that again. Look at me!" He grabbed her shoulder to turn her around. As she swung her head sharply in the opposite direction, she lost her balance. Her face slammed into the wall, knocking her unconscious.

Dexter looked at the still body, afraid that she was dead.

Toby and Wilbur saw the commotion as Toby was parking. They leaped from the car and sprinted to the railroad station. Dexter saw them coming and ran toward his car.

Wilbur yelled, "I'll get Dexter!"

Toby ran to Charla, knelt down beside her, and took her wrist. "Thank God, she has a pulse," he whispered. He was about to move her when he heard Dexter scream. He looked up to see that Wilbur had thrown him to the ground and was pounding Dexter's face with his fist. Blood was spurting from Dexter's nose.

Toby ran over and grabbed Wilbur by the shoulder. "That's enough. Stop hitting him."

Wilbur stood up and jerked Dexter to his feet. He said, "Don't worry about it. I nabbed him, and I'll get him to the car. You see if you can handle the girl."

Toby watched Wilbur strut to the car like a Bantam rooster. He saw that several people in the railroad station were watching, their jaws agape. Toby sighed.

Toby knelt down beside Charla and wiped blood off her chin. She opened her eyes. She asked, "Am I under arrest?"

Toby said, "Yes. But I'm going to take you to the hospital first."

CHAPTER 20

▼

After returning from the police station, Bill Boyd ate a light lunch and took a nap. He was now rested and getting bored. He tried to read a magazine but couldn't concentrate. He tossed the magazine down and paced the floor. He was startled when the phone rang.

He picked up the receiver.

"Bill, this is Ben Winchester from the *Sarnia Observer*. I have some information you'll find interesting. A friend of mine from the *Toronto Globe and Mail* just called to say that the Toronto police are looking for two young women who disappeared Saturday night. Their names are Soma Fekete and Zizi Balogh, and they migrated to Canada about a year ago. They fit the pattern we were talking about Sunday night."

"You mean they came to Canada without their families?"

Ben said, "Right. The police think the kidnappers might be smuggling them into the United States."

"Let's hope the women are found safe and sound."

"I'll call you if I hear anything else."

Bill said, "That would be great. Thanks for the information."

Bill walked to his desk and looked at the schedule of trains using the St. Clair Tunnel. He realized that the next train from Canada was due in twenty minutes. He put on his duster and goggles and ran to his car. Within minutes he was racing across Port Huron. He parked a block away from the railroad tracks and walked quickly toward the man he had hired to watch the tunnel.

"Hi, Henry. How are things going?"

Henry spit a spray of tobacco juice. "Not much traffic today."

"The next train is likely to be here in about fifteen minutes."

"I don't mind takin' your money, but I doubt if we're ever goin' to see anything."

Bill grinned. "Thanks for being honest."

As the two men paced back and forth, a horse-drawn carriage with its curtains shut pulled into the railroad grounds. When it stopped, a freight car stood between the carriage and Bill, blocking his sight.

Bill asked, "Can you see anything?"

"Nope."

"Let's get closer." The two men carefully made their way to the freight car. They peeked around the corner of the car just in time to see the railroad security man nod to the carriage before he walked across the tracks in the opposite direction. Bill whispered, "What's that all about?"

Henry replied, "Beats me, but it's the most action I've seen since I started this job."

Minutes later, the train from Toronto emerged from the tunnel. As soon as it came to a stop, the doors of one of the cars opened and a burly man jumped out. A smaller man handed him two young women. The women had coats thrown over their heads and shoulders, but it was apparent to Bill that their hands were tied behind their backs. The two men hustled their captives over to the carriage.

One woman was weeping and nearly had to be carried by the smaller man. The other woman walked with as much dignity as she could muster.

Bill said, "I can't believe it!"

"Looks like we've got ourselves a kidnapping. Let's go save them."

Henry began to move, but Bill grabbed his arm. He whispered, "No. Stay here."

Bill and Henry heard angry voices. The smaller man said, "You heard me. I'm never going to do this again. This job stinks."

A woman's voice said, "Don't be an ass, Charlie. Help Carl get those two women in this carriage right now!"

Charlie folded his arms across his chest and refused to move.

As Carl forced the two women in the other carriage, the woman snarled, "Then you can go to hell."

As soon as the carriage left the railroad yards, Bill and Henry ran to Bill's car. Bill said, "It looks like they're going downtown. Did you get a good look at the woman in the carriage?"

Henry said, "No, but it sounded like Velvet Cushion."

"That's what I thought. It's my guess they're headed for her house of pleasure. Did you recognize the men she called Charlie and Carl?"

"I never saw them before. What are we going to do now?"

Bill said, "When we get across the Black River, I'll drop you off. You run to the police station and tell them what's going on."

*   *   *   *

Mary and her friends walked briskly down Huron Avenue toward the Black River. The meeting with the Life-Saving Service had taken place as expected, but it was still disappointing.

Nancy said, "I still think they could have given us some help."

"Maybe," Mary said. "But they do have a lot of activities they are responsible for. And they don't have a very large budget."

Donna said, "I don't imagine we'll have any more luck when we talk to Customs."

Leah said, "At least we've got Bill Boyd helping us."

The four women had now reached Quay Street and were standing in front of Ballantine's Dry Goods Store when they saw a carriage with its curtains drawn cross the Black River and turn east onto Quay Street.

Nancy nodded at the carriage. "It's a pretty hot day to have all those curtains shut. It seems like they would want some air."

Bill's car also crossed the bridge and turned onto Quay Street. It stopped momentarily as Henry jumped out and dashed across the street to the women. He said, "Bill wants you to know we might have somethin'. I'm goin' to the police station to tell them about two women who were taken off the train just a few minutes ago."

Mary asked, "Where's Bill going?"

"We think the women are being taken to Velvet's house of pleasure."

Donna asked, "Where's that?"

Nancy said, "I know."

Henry frowned. "You women better stay away. This is a matter for the police." He turned and began running toward the police station.

Leah asked, "Are we going to do anything?"

Nancy said, "We might get in the way."

Mary looked at the other three. "I don't think it would be a problem if we just observed. Nancy, where is this place?"

"It's just down there a couple of blocks."

Mary said, "Then, let's go." She began walking down Quay Street.
The other women hesitated for a minute and then hurried after her.

*   *   *   *

Bill followed the carriage down Quay Street. He parked about a block away from Velvet's establishment and watched the occupants of the carriage enter a side door. He slouched down in his seat to wait for the police. Bill's eyes widened as he saw the large, muscular man he knew as Carl leave Velvet's and walk toward his car.

Carl stared down at Bill. "What you doing here?"

"Nothing. I'm just waiting for a friend."

Carl jerked open the car door and pulled Bill out. "Velvet wants to know why you're following us."

"Following you?"

Carl snarled, "Don't play dumb. We couldn't miss seein' that fancy red car of yours."

"But…"

Carl slapped Bill across the face. "But nothin'. Get movin'."

Carl pushed Bill through a side door and took him to a room on the second floor. Carl said, "Here he is."

Velvet looked up from her desk, "Good afternoon, Mr. Boyd. May I ask you why you followed us from the railroad and then parked outside?"

Bill looked at Velvet's cold, menacing stare. He knew that he could not deceive her. "I saw the two girls taken from the train. I have reason to believe you are involved in white slave trade."

Velvet stood up and walked around the desk. "I see." She turned to Carl. "You know what to do."

Carl spun Bill around and wrenched his right arm up against his back. Bill yelled, "Wait! The police are on their way."

"The cops?"

"Yes. I sent my assistant to the police station. They should be here any time."

Velvet said, "Carl can dispose of you and your car before they get here."

Using his left hand, Bill pointed out the window at Mary standing on the corner. "That woman knows I'm here."

Velvet laughed harshly. "You're not fooling anyone."

"I'm not kidding. She was the one who hired me to watch the railroad. If you look farther down the street, I bet you'll see others."

Velvet looked out the window and saw the other women walking back and forth. She glanced at Carl. "I don't know if he's lying or not, but we can't take a chance. It's time you and I disappeared." She quickly opened a wall safe, withdrew as much money as she could shove into a large bag, and fled down the stairs.

Carl pushed Bill to floor, kicked him in the ribs, and followed Velvet.

By the time Bill stood up and caught his breath, they were gone. Looking out the window, he could see Sergeant Williams and another patrolman on their bicycles, about two blocks away. He ran downstairs to open the front door.

"Velvet's getting away!"

Sergeant Williams skidded to a stop. "Where did she go?"

"I don't know. She's probably in a black carriage."

Mary ran over. "I saw it head east toward the St. Clair river."

Sergeant Williams ordered the patrolman to find the carriage. "I want you ladies to stay here." Motioning to Bill, he said, "You come inside and tell me about this kidnapping."

As Bill described what happened, they went from room to room, looking for the captives. Finally, in a room next to Velvet's office, they found the two women, wide-eyed and shaking with fear. Bill knelt down and untied them. He whispered softly, "It's over. You're going to be all right."

CHAPTER 21

▼

Toby rushed Charla into the hospital. A nurse looked up from her desk. She stood as soon as she saw Charla's bloodstained clothes. "Come this way, officer. Dr. Nelson will see her right away."

Within minutes Dr. Nelson was examining Charla, while Toby was escorted to the waiting room. Toby asked, "Can I use a phone? I need to call the police station."

"Certainly. It's there by the desk."

Sylvia answered the station's telephone.

Toby said, "Sylvia. I am at the hospital with Charla. Did Patrolman Greene bring in Dexter Conroy?"

Sylvia said, "Yes. They just came in a few minutes ago. What are you doing at the hospital?"

"Dexter threw Charla up against the wall. I don't know how badly she's hurt. I'm going to stay here to interview her if the doctor will let me. Then I want to come back to the station, but I don't know if I can bring Charla back with me. What should I do?"

"Wait just a minute."

Sylvia returned to the phone. "I just talked to Chief Chambers. He's going to send Patrolman Greene over to take your place. He said to come back to the station as soon as you can."

"OK." Toby put the receiver down and paced back and forth until he saw Dr. Nelson enter the waiting room. Toby asked, "How is she?"

Dr. Nelson said, "She has a broken nose, and the deep cut on her chin required several stitches. Fortunately, she doesn't appear to have any internal injuries."

Toby asked, "Can I see Charla? It's very important that I ask her some questions."

"Follow me."

Dr. Nelson stood at the end of the bed. "Charla, this young officer wants to ask you some questions."

Toby was shocked to see how Charla's once beautiful face had been disfigured. It was now swollen, bruised, and bandaged. Her hair looked like someone had cut it with a lawn mower. Charla lay with her eyes closed.

Toby asked, "Charla, can you hear me?"

Charla opened her eyes and nodded.

Toby asked, "Why did Dexter want to hurt you?"

"It's a long story. Let's just say he's got a temper like his dad, and I got to experience it from both of them."

"Why were you trying to leave town?"

"I didn't want to be arrested for the murder of Conroy. I just wanted to get away."

"Did you kill Conroy?"

"No."

"Do you know who did?"

Charla grimaced as she shook her head no.

Toby asked, "Why did you have Luke Laboy break into the hotel rooms?"

"Luke?"

"Yes. We caught him breaking into a house. He admitted he broke into the two hotels for you."

Carla said, "Please don't punish that kid. I talked him into it. I was looking for something that belonged to me."

"Were you looking for the pictures that Edgar Reynolds took of you when you were younger?"

Carla's eyes flashed with anger. "Yes. I found six of them. But that ass must have hidden one of them someplace else."

"Do you know we arrested him for the murder of Dexter Conroy?"

"I saw him in handcuffs earlier today. Reynolds is the one I wish was dead. He ruined my life."

Toby said, "That's all the questions for now, but please don't try to leave town. You are under arrest for breaking and entering. There will be a policeman outside your room as long as you're in the hospital."

Charla sighed and closed her eyes.

*   *   *   *

Toby drove back to the police station. As he was about to enter the building, Detective Gressley greeted him at the door. "Tobias, I'm glad you're back. We have a search warrant for Conroy's house. I'll fill you in on the interviews with Mr. Reynolds and Dexter Conroy on the way."

They got into the Ford car and drove onto Huron Avenue. Gressley asked, "How is Charla?"

"She has a broken nose and lots of scratches on her face. One deep cut on her chin required several stitches."

"Did you get a chance to talk to her?"

Toby said, "Yes. She claims she didn't kill Conroy and doesn't know who did. She admitted to breaking into the hotel rooms looking for the pictures Reynolds took of her. What did you learn from Reynolds and Dexter?"

"Let me tell you about the good Mr. Reynolds first. In his attempt to prove he did not murder Dexter Conroy, he gave us lots of good information. He thought we had the seven nude pictures he had taken of Charla when she was fifteen. Reynolds explained that Mr. Conroy got possession of them and was going to blackmail Reynolds into giving him an advantage in the road construction projects."

Toby asked, "How did that happen?"

"It seems that Conroy and Reynolds met three weeks ago in Lansing at a meeting about Michigan's roads. Conroy offered a bribe but Reynolds refused. His comment to me was something like, 'I might have unorthodox views about art, but I am an honest government official.' Despite the bribe refusal, the two seemed to get along. They went out for drinks. One thing led to another until Reynolds invited Conroy to his house to see his collection of nude photos. Conroy seemed to share Reynolds' interest until he saw the photos of Charlotte Clemon. Conroy must have realized that Charla and Charlotte was the same person. Later, Reynolds realized that Charlotte's pictures were missing.

"About a week ago, Conroy called Reynolds. He said that he would return the photos if he would give him favorable consideration on the concrete contracts for any roads built in the Thumb area. He told Reynolds that he would bring the pictures to Port Huron this week. They were to have had a secret meeting Sunday. Reynolds said he wanted to see the photos to make sure Conroy had them. When Reynolds went to the meeting, Conroy didn't show up."

Toby asked, "Then how did he get the photos if he didn't murder Conroy?"

"He received a note Sunday from Dexter Jr. saying that he had the pictures. He would return them if Reynolds would give him $2,000. Yesterday, Reynolds had a Lansing bank wire a money order so he could buy the pictures."

"Was Dexter going to use the money to cover his gambling debts?"

Gressley said, "I'm guessing that's why Dexter wanted the money."

"How do we know Reynolds is telling the truth?"

"I don't know if it's all true, but he did show me a copy of a money order. And he said he was angry when he got back to the hotel and discovered there were only six photos in the envelope."

Toby asked, "Do you think Jr. kept one to blackmail Reynolds a second time?"

"That's what Reynolds thinks."

"What did Dexter say?"

Gressley said, "Absolutely nothing. He just stared at me though the entire interview. So that's why we need to do a thorough search of the Conroy house. Somehow Dexter got his hands on the photographs."

"Do you think he would actually murder his own father to get the pictures so he could blackmail Reynolds?"

"It's a strong possibility. That's why we need to go back to the Conroy house."

Mrs. Conroy was working in her garden when the touring car came to a stop in her driveway. She stood up and wiped her hands on her stained gardening frock as the two police officers approached her. Gressley said, "Good morning, Mrs. Conroy. Your flowers look beautiful."

Mrs. Conroy smiled wanly, her tired, bloodshot eyes not making contact with Gressley's. She spoke morosely. "What do you want?"

Gressley showed her the warrant. "We have reason to believe that we will find important evidence about your husband's murder, either in the house or in the garage. You may come with us if you like."

Without looking directly at either policeman, Mrs. Conway went back to her work. She shrugged her shoulders. "Do what you have to do."

As the policemen walked toward the house, Gressley said, "She certainly appears to be in a gloomy mood today."

Toby agreed, "She seems a lot worse than when we were here yesterday. Do you think she's in greater mourning now that the shock of her husband's death has worn off?"

"Perhaps."

Mrs. Conroy watched the two men as they walked toward the house. Then she turned and knelt in front of a rosebush. She cupped her hands around a blossom and breathed in the sweet flagrance. With a sudden, powerful movement, she ripped the flower from the bush and threw it on the ground.

The policemen entered the house. Gressley said, "Let's start with Dexter Jr.'s bedroom." They found the room on the second floor, near the stairs.

Toby opened a dresser drawer. He picked up an envelope and looked inside. "Here's an envelope with a lot of money in it. There's also a receipt showing that $2,000 was transferred into Dexter's account yesterday and then withdrawn later that same day."

After spending a few more minutes checking the room closely, they went downstairs to the living room. Gressley asked, "Do you notice anything different about the fireplace mantel?"

"The wedding picture that I commented on yesterday is gone. She sure got rid of that in a hurry. Maybe she decided to throw it away after we talked to her about Mr. Conroy's mistresses."

Gressley said, "Let's check out the kitchen." Toby looked at the kitchen knives while Gressley rummaged through the wastebasket.

Gressley said, "Here's the wedding picture, as well as several others of Mr. Conroy. They're all ripped to shreds." He dug deeper in the basket. "Tobias, look at this."

Toby looked at the envelope in Gressley's hand. "Isn't it just an ordinary business envelope?"

"The envelope's ordinary but not its contents." He withdrew a photograph of a nude girl. "Doesn't this look like it could be Charla when she was younger?"

"Sure does. That must be the missing picture Mr. Reynolds and Charla were talking about."

Gressley said, "Put all of this evidence into your investigating kit. We need to ask Mrs. Conroy some more questions."

As the two men were about to open the kitchen door, they saw Mrs. Conroy carrying a large can of clippings toward the garage.

Gressley said, "She sure is a strong woman. Look how easily she's handling that heavy load. If she can do that, she would have had the strength to move her husband's dead body."

They were both surprised when Mrs. Conroy threw the can against the garage, spilling the contents. Then she turned and walked quickly back to the rose garden.

Toby pointed at the rosebushes. "Look at that. All of the rosebushes have been stripped of their flowers."

Gressley said, "We better be careful. It looks like she could be dangerous."

Toby nodded solemnly.

The two policemen approached Mrs. Conroy. Gressley said, "We're done checking the house. We need to look inside the garage. Is it locked?"

Mrs. Conroy's eyes glistened with a strange brightness. "Yes. The key is in my basket with my garden tools."

Toby pointed to a basket near his feet. "Is that it? I'll get the key for you."

Mrs. Conroy shouted, "No! I'll get it!" She opened the basket's lid and reached in. She withdrew a key and handed it to Gressley.

Gressley accepted the key. "Thanks. We took a few things from the house. We have $2,000 from Dexter's room, as well as an envelope containing a picture of a nude girl that we found in the kitchen wastebasket."

Mrs. Conroy looked confused. "Just one picture?"

Gressley said, "Yes. We believe Dexter murdered his father and then used other nude photos of that girl to blackmail Mr. Reynolds."

"Dexter? You think Dexter killed his father?"

"Yes, we have him in jail now." Gressley began walking toward the garage.

Mrs. Conroy's eyes blazed. "You fool. Dexter didn't kill anyone." She reached once more for the garden basket.

Gressley turned to face Mrs. Conroy. He asked, "Is there something else you want to tell us?"

Mrs. Conroy said nothing, but when she removed her hand from the basket, she was gripping a pruning knife, stained with blood. Before the startled policemen could respond, she lunged at Toby. As he put his hand to protect himself, the sharp blade slashed his forearm.

Gressley grabbed her wrist and twisted it until she dropped the knife. As the knife tumbled to the ground, Mrs. Conroy tore at his face with her fingernails.

When Gressley pulled her hand away from his face, she wrenched free and began running toward the garage.

Toby tackled her and brought her arms around behind her back.

Gressley ran over and handcuffed her.

Toby ripped off his jacket to find that the wound, although bloody, was superficial. Gressley tied his handkerchief around Toby's arm. Gressley said, "I think that should be OK until we have a doctor examine it."

Gressley and Toby turned to look at the enraged expression on Mrs. Conroy's face. Gressley said, "Well, Tobias. What is your opinion about the physical capabilities of women now?"

CHAPTER 22

▼

John Gressley walked slowly along the beach at Lakeside Park. The weather was in the midseventies with low humidity and a pleasant northerly wind blowing across Lake Huron. It was a welcome relief to the hot, muggy days Port Huron residents had just experienced. Gressley remembered the first time he tried to swim in the lake. He was used to small, warm inland lakes and was shocked with how cold the water was in the middle of the summer.

He was fascinated with how the lake seemed to change its personality. Today it had a sensual nature as the waves repeatedly caressed the shore and then receded. Other times the lake was quiet and reserved with its surface as smooth as glass. Occasionally it would demonstrate its anger, as huge waves would batter the shoreline. When combined with snow in late fall, these storms could be disastrous.

He watched the sailboats skimming gracefully over the water. He admired the skill it must take to sail. He also looked for seashells as he walked the beach. Toby told him that his son was collecting them. Since the Sharpes had invited him to a picnic today to celebrate Toby's first year on the police force, he thought it might be nice to give Chris some shells.

Gressley allowed his mind to reflect on the recent murder case. Dexter Conroy Jr.'s refusal to talk immediately after his arrest was a futile attempt to protect his mother. After Mrs. Conroy was arrested, her son explained that he found the photos of Charla in the wastebasket. He knew that his father had the photos and had a pretty good idea that he was using them to blackmail Mr. Reynolds. Dexter guessed that the only way the photos would have been in his home is that his mother removed them from his father's body after she killed him.

Mrs. Conroy admitted that Dexter's conjectures were true. When asked why she didn't throw the photos in the lake, she said she didn't know what they were until she got home. She thought the envelope might have had some important information about the business. She didn't know her son had found them.

Charla was allowed to leave as soon as her injuries healed, the scar across her chin detracting significantly from her beauty. Once the police found out what Charla experienced as a teenager, all charges were dropped. Gressley could not imagine the psychological scars burdening that young woman.

Gressley looked up and saw the Sharpe family emerging from the bathhouse. He waved and walked over to greet them. He showed Chris the shells. "Look at what I've got for you."

"Oh boy, thanks! Daddy and I are going to make a sand fort. I'll put these on top."

"Yeah," said Toby. "That's going to be my main job this morning."

"You two go ahead then. I'll enjoy talking to your wife for a while." Gressley spread a blanket on the beach and they sat down.

Amanda grabbed Mary's hand. "Mommy, me want candy."

"Sorry, honey. You can't have candy now. We'll have some after our lunch."

"Mommy, me want lunch now."

Laughing, Mary handed Amanda a toy shovel and said, "In a little bit. For now, why don't you go play in the sand with Daddy and Chris?"

As Amanda waddled toward the water, waving her shovel, Mary turned to John. "You must be pleased with the way the Conroy and Reynolds cases turned out."

"Yes. And Toby did a good job."

Mary asked, "So he did turn out to be 'trainable?'"

Gressley chucked. "That word might have been a little harsh. But at the time, I was trying to challenge him."

Mary said, "You did a good job of that. It meant a lot to him that you picked him to work on the murder case." After a moment's pause, she said, "I thought Sylvia and Bill were going to come today."

"They'll be here soon. Bill agreed to give Sylvia driving lessons. Her newest idea is that if she knows how to drive, it might be of some value at the station."

"I wish her luck."

Gressley said, "Mary, I want you know that I was a little skeptical of that scheme you and your friends devised at the St. Clair River Tunnel. But your action saved those poor girls from a terrible fate."

"But I regretted that I put Bill at risk. He might have been killed."

"You didn't put Bill at risk. He volunteered to do it. And with all the praise he received from the newspaper article he wrote, I'm sure he's happy you asked him to get involved."

Mary said, "I guess you're right. What will happen to those poor women who were smuggled into Port Huron?"

"They seem to be recovering from their experience. The doctors at the hospital said that even Soma has improved considerably. They plan to return to Toronto in a couple of weeks."

"Toby mentioned something about them getting some money that was found at Velvet's establishment."

Gressley nodded. "Yes. In her haste to escape, she left about $5,000 in the safe. City officials have decided that Soma and Zizi deserve it as much as anyone. Bill thinks Velvet shoved about ten times that amount into a bag."

"And she's never been found?"

"No. Her carriage was found along the river. We think that somehow she managed to escape into Canada. But nobody has any clue where Velvet Cushion is now."

Mary asked, "Did they ever catch any of the men?'

"The Toronto police found the one called Nikki. He explained how he would find young women who had come to Canada alone. Carl and Charlie would kidnap the women and deliver them to Velvet Cushion. She sold them to a man in Chicago who would force them to marry men out west."

Mary shook her head in disbelief.

Gressley picked up a package he had placed on the blanket and handed it to Mary. "I bought you a thank-you gift for inviting me today."

Mary opened the package, and smiled in delight. "It's Willa Cather's new book, *O Pioneers*. I've been looking forward to reading this. Thank you very much."

"You're welcome. Toby suggested that it might be a good choice."

Laying the book in her lap, Mary said, "What's going to happen to Mrs. Conroy?"

"I imagine she'll be placed in an institution for the insane. According to her son, her behavior was becoming increasingly erratic. He encouraged her to consume alcohol because it seemed to calm her down."

"What about Dexter?"

"He'll probably spend some time in jail for blackmail."

"What kind of punishment will Mr. Reynolds get for taking those terrible pictures?"

"I'm afraid he received his punishment last night."

Mary raised her eyebrows. "Already?"

"I received a call this morning from Hugh Leffets of the Lansing police, so Toby doesn't even know this yet. Reynolds' body was found this morning. Someone knocked him out and strangled him with silk stockings. The stockings were embroidered with snakes. A rope was arranged in an oval on a bed sheet, with the body placed in the middle. When you approached the body, it resembled a photograph in a picture frame."

Mary felt shivers go through her spine. She glanced at Toby playing affectionately with their children and reflected on the seemingly unlimited human capacity for love and hatred, for greed and compassion.

Mary said, "I noticed that you've been calling my husband Toby today. Haven't you always called him Tobias?"

"Toby asked me to stop using Tobias. His involvement in the murder investigation has changed him. He seems more confident and assertive than he did a month ago."

"It's interesting that you would mention change. I've been thinking about how much our country has changed in the last thirty years. I'm sure you've noticed a significant change during your life."

Gressley focused his gaze on Lake Huron as he considered Mary's comment. The sun's rays were causing the water to sparkle like diamonds. He said, "I agree. It seems like we're experiencing a change in eras. Let's hope it's for the better."

Chronology of historical facts

1913

- Port Huron's professional baseball team finished third in the Border League. The league disbanded at the end of the season.

- In November, the Great Lakes experienced its greatest storm in recorded history. Eight ships sank in Lake Huron, drowning nearly 200 men. The *Charles S. Price* lies in about sixty feet of water ten miles north of Port Huron.

1914

- Havers Motors' factory burned down, forcing the company out of business. One of its cars is owned by the Port Huron Museum.

- Archduke Francis Ferdinand, heir to the Austrian throne, was assassinated, triggering World War I.

- Port Huron changed the name of Butler Street to Grand River Avenue.

1915

- The United States Life-Saving Service changed its name to the United States Coast Guard.

- *The Birth of a Nation*, based on Thomas Dixon's novel *The Clansman*, was released. The movie's blatantly racist message contributed to a rise in membership in the Ku Klux Klan.

1917

- The Folmer and Schwing Department of Eastman Kodak Company produced the Graflex fingerprint camera, the first commercial fingerprint camera in the United States.

1919

- Michigan issued its first driver's license.

1920

- The American Professional Football Association was founded. Its name was changed to the National Football League in 1922.

- Women's suffrage was granted.

- The Second Maccabees' Temple was converted to the Algonquian Hotel. The hotel was destroyed by fire in 2000.

1922

- The Port Huron police department purchased its first car.

1923

- Sperry's moved from 242 Huron Avenue to 301 Huron Avenue. Sperry's closed in 2000. The building is now occupied by the House of Denmark Furniture Store.

1930

- The interurban stopped running.

1933

- The Port Huron police department equipped its first car with a radio.

1936

- The *Tashmoo* sunk when it hit a rock. No one was drowned. The *Tashmoo* was elected to the National Maritime Hall of Fame in 1985.

- According to the *Port Huron Times-Herald* (April 13, 1936), Helen R. Hoffman was Port Huron's first regular policewoman. Although her primary assignment was police matron, she apparently assumed other responsibilities. For example, another *Times-Herald* article (January 8, 1942) reported that she was the first Port Huron woman licensed by the Federal Communications Commission Department in Detroit to "receive and broadcast messages over the short wave police radio."

1958

- The Majestic Theater was torn down. The area where it stood is now called the Majestic parking lot.

1982

- The Hotel Harrington was placed on the National Register of Historical Buildings. It has been a facility for the elderly since 1989.

1993

- Work began on a new St. Clair Tunnel. The one-hundred-year-old tunnel had become too small for modern rail cars. A new tunnel opened in 1995.

Additional tidbits

- A complete set (sixteen) of 1913 T-200 Fatima baseball cards in near mint condition is worth $25,000.

- The recipe for Kern's Cream of America beer was purchased by the Quay Street Brewery. It is now called Michigan Cream.

- The Fort Gratiot Lighthouse is Michigan's oldest continually operational lighthouse. It was named a historical site in 1971 by the Michigan Historical Commission.

- The Ladies of the Maccabees of the World is now called the Woman's Life Insurance Society. It continues to provide many financial services for women and men. Its national office is still located in Port Huron.

- Currently, the St. Clair County Road Commission is responsible for over 1,500 miles of roads, of which 565 are paved. This does not include the hundreds of miles of state highways, interstate highways or any streets in incorporated cities and villages that exist in St. Clair County.

Final notes

The following places are fictional: Fisherman's Tavern, Hotel Marion, Velvet Cushion's house of pleasure, Mrs. Jenkins' boardinghouse, *Port Huron Star* newspaper office, and Prince Albert Hotel. All of the other places mentioned on the map actually existed in 1913.

Everybody and everything mentioned in the following list were in Port Huron in 1913: Burton Baker, Captain of the *Tashmoo*; Charles Bailey, St. Clair County Road Commission Chairman; C. Kern Brewing Company; Dan Patch; Detroit United Railway; Frank Kimball, keeper of the Fort Gratiot Lighthouse; George Chambers, Port Huron police chief; Halton Powell, vaudeville performer; J. B. Petit Company; Kern's cream of America beer; Louis Corbat, minor league baseball player; Lucy Hendricks, president of the Port Huron Ladies Library Association; Port Huron's Chautauqua week; Port Huron Ladies Library Association; Port Huron Men's Association; Port Huron's minor league baseball team; *Port Huron Times Herald*; St. Clair County Road Commission; St. Clair River Tunnel; *Tashmoo*; the Ladies of the Maccabees of the World; U.S. Life-Saving Service; and Vernors ginger ale.

The Port Huron police department did not have the rank of detective in 1913. I invented a fictional rank for an equally fictional character.

All of the other characters are imaginary. Any resemblance between the fictional characters and anyone, living or dead, is purely coincidental. Some dates, times, and locations have been slightly altered to facilitate the story.

978-0-595-37216-4
0-595-37216-3